# ECHOES IN THE NIGHT

CULT OF THE ENDLESS NIGHT SERIES

BOOK 4

IAN FORTEY
AND
RON RIPLEY

EDITED BY ANNE LAO
AND DAWN KLEMISH

ISBN: 9798867527662
Copyright © 2023 by ScareStreet.com

All rights reserved. This book or any portion thereof may not be reproduced or used in any manner whatsoever without written permission from the publisher except for the use of brief quotations in a book review.

*This is a work of fiction. Any resemblance to actual persons, living or dead, or actual events is purely coincidental.*

# Thank You and Bonus Novel!

We'd like to take a moment to thank you for your ongoing support. You make this all possible! To really show you our appreciation for purchasing this book, **we'd love to send you a full-length horror novel in 3 formats (MOBI, EPUB and PDF) absolutely free!**

Download your full-length horror novel, get free short stories, and receive future discounts by visiting www.ScareStreet.com

See you in the shadows,
Team Scare Street

# Prologue

The echo through the tunnel sounded like the painful moan of a lumbering beast. It was low and thunderous but muffled through seemingly endless concrete and steel. The chilled air of the dark, damp space dulled it further, making it flat and droning.

Leon knew the sound was nothing to fear. It was a train in a distant tunnel, rattling down the tracks between stations. It was just close enough that its rumble could be heard in the abandoned tunnels around Tremont where he'd made his home.

The Tremont Street subway line had not been Leon's first choice of homes when he ventured out on his own in Boston. He was raised in Lower Mills, and his dad had died when he was twelve, killed in a gas station robbery when he was trying to buy a Snickers bar and a scratch-off ticket after work.

Leon's mom had worked a couple of jobs and was rarely home, and as a kid, he faulted her for that every chance he got. Falling in with what his grandma called "the wrong crowd" had been easy, the drugs, easier. Ruining his life, the easiest of all.

He hadn't spoken to his mother in more than five years because each was as stubborn as the other and he couldn't handle her judgment. Better to go it alone, even if that meant living in the tunnels of an abandoned subway.

*It sounds worse than it is*, he told himself. Tremont was the oldest subway line in America. Much of it was still in use, but the southern tunnel had been closed off for years. He was living in history. Living in it with rats, the cold, and guys who'd stab you for five dollars if they thought they could get away with it.

If he stayed in the right tunnels, things were better. There was a community of people down there who were rough around the edges, but they weren't maniacs. They were good people forced into dangerous circumstances, same as anywhere. But they looked out for each other when they could, in the ways they could. It wasn't a hippie commune, but people shared food and water when they had extra. One guy even gave him a blanket on his first night.

Leon made his living, such as it was, pickpocketing tourists. He'd learned some sleight of hand from his dad when he was a kid and parlayed that into some deft finger work in his teens. Nine times out of ten, he could slip a wallet from some idiot's pocket while they were snapping photos outside of Fenway. The tenth time, he just had to be faster so his mark wouldn't catch him.

He made enough to keep himself fed and clothed. And high. Some days were better than others, sure. Some months, too. But it was the bed he had made, and he was making the best of it.

Mapping the passageways had been the hardest part. It would be easier if he could get in and out of the underground tunnels at different points. Almost everyone in Tremont used the same entrance, and a couple had found what they called the Back Door for emergency use. That was how everyone ducked out when cops came, or when someone got too violent.

Having two entrances within a small space was too suspicious, Leon thought. It drew too much attention. He didn't want anyone to see where he lived or how to get there. So he started mapping the tunnels wherever he could. Traveling the dark, lonely passages looking for signs of light and access points that let him slip in and out across the city.

He'd found a dozen ways to get into active tunnels and slip into and out of stations that were still in use. He'd also found a couple more abandoned places he could sneak through.

He wanted more city-wide access though, places he could go into no matter where he was that would allow him to make his way back to the southern Tremont tunnel he called home. Being invisible had its perks, and if he could outsmart the cops, it would be all the better.

The big issue with mapping the world below in unused places was light. There was always a risk of discovery in the tunnels, with transit cops and regular cops and random strangers who had their reasons for hiding in secret places. He didn't want to risk using light until he knew he was safe. A flashlight put a target on his back for anyone present, so he would often navigate unknown places by feel and sound and whatever ambient light might have come in through cracks and grates.

That morning, he had discovered a collapsed wall section that took him through to tunnels he'd never seen. He wasn't even sure where in the city it was. South somewhere, but under what section of the city, he couldn't say. Not every tunnel was an old subway tunnel: some were access tunnels used in the system's construction, or auxiliary pathways. He'd even stumbled upon the odd rest areas the original builders must have used, complete with musty cots and card tables and kitchenettes.

The new tunnel was colder than the others he was familiar with, and the echoes came through louder. He didn't let it rattle him because there was no reason for it to do so. The sounds were just trains. The cold was just because he was underground. There was nothing to fear.

Leon had heard stories from others in Tremont, about something that lived in the tunnels with them. Something that crept out of the shadows now and then to take people away. He didn't believe a word of it, of course.

By nature, transient people were not committed to staying in one place. That people from an abandoned subway tunnel were never seen again meant nothing. They could have moved on to greener pastures. Or gone to shelters or jail, or maybe even died. It was harsh but true, and it didn't need a supernatural explanation. Anyone who died in those tunnels was more likely to have overdosed or been beaten by some random psycho.

Leon had never believed the stories, even if a handful of others were sold on them. He knew life was hard and terrifying enough, without having to make up boogeymen. Ghosts and monsters were just coping mechanisms for the broken people who couldn't handle the reality of life. Nothing was fair, the universe didn't cut anyone a break, and death was a Snickers and a scratch-off lottery ticket away from anyone.

Putting the faint twinge of fear he felt in his gut out of his mind, Leon stumbled slowly through the dark, his hand running along the cold, damp brick to his right. If the tunnel paid off, it would get him at least twelve blocks farther south than any of the other passageways, he was sure. That was good coverage and would be valuable in a pinch.

The cold air was stale, and there was something both earthy and greasy about it. Like fungus growing in motor oil, maybe. Even that wasn't entirely unusual. And was preferable to some of the more populated tunnels. Many of those smelled of urine, body odor, and worse.

Leon's feet splashed through puddles, the water soaking through the canvas of his shoes and chilling him even more. Little splashes echoed along with the rumbling of distant trains. In other tunnels, he would often hear the squeaks of rats or a distant conversation that traveled along the stone walls from somewhere far away. This place offered none of that. Beyond the mechanical echoes, there were no signs of life.

Then his foot snagged on something. Maybe an errant brick or some piece of trash. He stumbled and cursed, hands out to break his fall, as his knees smashed down onto the cold, wet brick.

Shaking his head and suppressing a growl, Leon sat up on his haunches and reached into his pocket. There was no one there. He was just being stupid by navigating in the dark. The tunnel had been opened after some kind of collapse, after all. No one was down there.

He pulled out a small flashlight. If he saw a junction or an exit, he'd shut it off. But he had no intention of continuing to stumble blindly through a tunnel that could end with him breaking his neck.

The flashlight came to light with a click. Its soft, yellow beam illuminated the floor of the tunnel before him, immersed in an inch of water and made up of stained yellow and brown stone, strewn with bits of broken rock and clutter.

The chill in the air grew stronger. One hand still on the brick wall to his right, Leon held the flashlight as steady as he could. The circle of yellow light it cast wavered as he stared at the shallow puddle of water just at the edge of the light's reach.

His hand shook. The beam shuddered though he tried to hold the flashlight steady. Before him, partially immersed in the shallow water, was a pair of bare feet the color of eggshells and lined with patches of deep purple. The nail was missing from the left big toe, exposing raw, rotten meat beneath. The other nails were too long and curved, like talons, cracked at the edges.

Leon didn't move. He couldn't, but he also didn't want to. All he had to do was lift the beam of light and follow it with his eyes. All he had to do was look up and see who was standing before him. But he could not.

The rumbling of the train faded in the distance until he was no longer sure if he could still hear it or whether it was just the memory of the sound that filled the silence. But soon even that was gone and there was nothing outside of himself. Only his rapid, shaky breathing broke through.

He willed himself to be calm as his breath formed wispy clouds before his face. But both his body and mind refused to listen. The light in his hand shook as though he had been taken by tremors, and he let out a soft whimper. The fear in his gut had become palpable, a living thing. He couldn't explain it, nor could he escape it.

In his mind, he knew there was nothing to fear. There was no monster in the tunnels, no ghost. There was no such thing there or anywhere. He knew that. And yet, he was still frozen, still unable to look up at whoever stood before him. Whatever stood there.

"Please," he whispered at last. He argued with himself in his head but he knew his rational mind was losing ground. He knew nothing. He didn't believe in ghosts because he had never seen one. He'd never seen Paris, either, had he? Never experienced a lot of things that were still very real.

Then the feet moved. They shuffled backward in the shuddering light, receding from the yellow sphere, and returning to darkness. They made no sound and caused no ripples in the water.

Seconds passed. Leon's breath evened out and his hold on the flashlight strengthened. His pulse slowed until finally, he felt himself able to move again. Hesitantly, he lifted his head, extending the beam of the flashlight down the length of the passage. There was nothing to see.

Leon sighed a long and shuddering breath and used the wall to support himself as he got to his feet. He ran a hand across his face, feeling beads of cold sweat, and shook his head.

"Jesus…" he muttered, taking a step forward.

An arm encircled him from behind, the hand the same eggshell and purple color, the fingernails ragged and curled into gray and black claws.

Leon called for help, but the hand clamped over his mouth. The flesh was like ice, so cold that it burned his lips. The pressure muffled his scream even as the thing pulled him backward. The flashlight fell from his grasp, smashing on the brick that had tripped him. Darkness swallowed everything, and only the sound of Leon's feet kicking into the shallow puddle filled the space.

Even that only lasted a moment.

# Chapter 1
# For the Wicked

Carl sat next to Shane and stared out into the backyard of the house. Neither had said anything for some time. Shane smoked, exhaling a cloud into the faint breeze that took it away. Somewhere in the distance, a driver slammed on their car horn in one sustained burst.

"It seems like a nice day today," Carl said in German. Shane grunted. It was sunny but rather cool, not that Carl could tell such things. As a ghost, he had little sense of ambient temperature.

"Nice enough," Shane agreed. Their small talk had become odd since Carl's kidnapping. The ghost seemed off somehow but refused to speak about or acknowledge it, and Shane was just as happy to let him work out his issues in his own time and way.

It had been a couple of months since the incident in Louisiana. Carl had been taken from the house by a ghost named Thomas Coulson, a psychic and telekinetic who straddled a mysterious line between life and death.

Coulson could pass for a living person. He could interact with the living, had a body that looked and felt physical, the whole bit. But he had been dead for some time and using his powers to hold himself together. The result was that he was untouchable by ghosts and though Shane had fought him once, it had been less than successful. Coulson was powerful and unique and terrifying.

Fortunately for all involved, Coulson was not keen on killing

Shane. He'd been coerced into helping the Endless Night to save the woman he loved. He and Shane had worked together to solve that problem and put an end to one of the most powerful members of the cult.

Shane had heard nothing from the group since he'd returned to Nashua. He had already left the cell that controlled New England in disarray, and the ones in the South, at least through Florida, were without leaders as well.

There was no way to know how many cells were in the Endless Night or how many members remained. They were a cult of rich and powerful people who traded in spirits and used them to secure more wealth and power, even if that required stealing and killing. But they had suffered great losses by involving Shane and Coulson. Hopefully, they had learned their lesson.

Carl had not handled being kidnapped well. Coulson had broken into the house on Berkley Street and taken Carl's remains hostage. The ghosts were powerless against Coulson and all of them had been affected by that, not just Carl. But Carl was the one who suffered the most. He had been sealed in a lead box and transported across the country. Shane understood how powerless that probably made him feel.

So, his old friend had changed. He was a little more withdrawn, and less talkative than normal. Shane felt confident it was just something he needed time with. He'd been a ghost for many years and had never dealt with a situation like that. Ghosts, in Shane's experience, were not easily adaptable to new situations. Not ones over which they had no control.

Shane had smoked the cigarette nearly to the filter when the phone rang, giving him a reason to do something other than sit and be quiet with Carl.

"Shane," James Moran said when Shane answered.

The Endless Night had put James through the ringer, forcing him into hiding and ultimately kidnapping him as well. Unlike Carl, though, James seemed no worse for the wear after his experience even though he'd been beaten by his captors.

"James, how are you holding up?"

Shane had only been to see the man once since they returned, figuring he would need time to heal and get over the experience. The bruises had faded by that time, but James seemed in good spirits and was back in the swing of things as though his abduction and near death had been a minor inconvenience.

"Well enough," the older man answered. "How is Carl?"

"Well enough," Shane replied. He had shared no information with James; it wasn't his place to do something like that. It seemed like gossip anyway, and he wasn't inclined to care for or take part in anything of the sort.

"Have you heard from Coulson?"

"No," Shane said.

He hoped he never heard from Coulson again. They had worked together to do a job, and that was as far as that needed to go. Coulson was powerful in a way that Shane was not comfortable with. He seemed decent enough, but the cult had manipulated him into doing its dirty work. If something like that happened again, or if one day Coulson just got fed up with the world, then the havoc he could cause would be unheard of.

Shane did not think he could stop Coulson if push came to shove. He didn't know of anyone who could. Coulson had no haunted item that could be sealed away or destroyed, and he was almost invulnerable to attack. As far as Shane was concerned, life would be better with Coulson far away for the rest of time.

"Jillian tells me she and Coulson went to some small town Oregon to get back to work with Sight Unseen. Seems like everything has been quiet since their return," James explained.

"You're in contact then," Shane said.

"Yes, of course. Jillian is a fascinating person. And Coulson also, though he and I haven't spoken formally."

"Right."

"But that is not the reason for my call. I have been looking into the Endless Night since Louisiana and have learned some interesting information."

Shane lit another cigarette and stared out at the yard. He could hear the change in James' voice, a nearly palpable sense of excitement. He wasn't afraid or nervous; he was thrilled.

"They all died in a bus crash?" Shane joked.

James chuckled.

"That would be karmic justice, I suppose. No, I have learned that there has recently been a great exodus in the area. New Hampshire, Massachusetts, Maine, Connecticut, everywhere that had been overseen by Randall West. It seems many an influential millionaire and business mogul has found a reason to move on to greener pastures."

"That a fact?" Shane asked.

"It is," James replied. "Anyone known to have links to the Endless Night or Randall West is gone."

Shane inhaled and held the smoke for a moment.

"You don't believe they're really gone, do you?"

"Not at all," James said, "but I believe they are significantly weakened. The top of the food chain fled when it became clear no one was safe. Whether they come back or settle elsewhere is another matter. But for now, this area has been gutted of their influence."

"Guess I should have a celebratory drink."

"Indeed. I'm not saying you toppled the entire cult, but I believe you did significant damage. And now, should they try to return and re-establish anything, we are better positioned to know about it."

"That's good," Shane responded. "I appreciate you keeping an eye on it."

"I'm not letting these people get the upper hand with me again." The older man's voice was grim and hinted at unspoken threats. Shane didn't blame him in the least. As it was, anyone left alive in the Endless Night was lucky Coulson hadn't torn through them.

"Any news on Florida?" Shane asked. He and Coulson had left the leader of the Florida cell, a man named Finley, to his fate in the dungeon he'd created to imprison spirits. He might have survived, even though there was no way to escape.

"I have fewer contacts down that way. Mr. Finley has not been seen, of course. I hear things are disorganized, however."

"Disorganized," Shane repeated with a laugh. "I can settle for that, I guess."

"I have heard that there are still some low-ranking individuals who are trying to fill the void," James continued. "At least locally. Nothing worth fretting over just yet, more of a 'who's president of the club now?' situation."

"What do you mean by low-level?" Shane asked.

"If you recall the Martells, I would consider them mid-level," James answered.

The Martells were a clueless husband and wife who posed as ghost collectors as a desperate status symbol. They were fools, but so were many of the cult members that Shane had met. If someone on the totem pole lower than them was trying to organize the remains of the cult, it seemed unlikely there was anything to be worried about.

"Bottom of the barrel," Shane said.

"Looks that way," James agreed. "If I learn anything new, I'll keep you informed."

"Appreciate it," Shane said, exhaling another puff of smoke. They said their goodbyes, and he hung up the phone, glancing at Carl.

"That was James Moran," he said.

"I heard," Carl answered. "The cult has been crippled. That is good to know."

"Yeah," Shane agreed. "Local rich idiots will have to come up with another unscrupulous way to make money and murder their rivals."

"I'm sure they already have a few plans in motion."

Carl fell silent again and Shane finished another cigarette before his phone interrupted their silent reverie once more.

"You are popular today," the ghost remarked.

"Belle of the ball." Shane grinned, looking at his phone. The call was from an unknown number.

He pressed the button to answer and held the phone to his ear.

"It's not getting better," a voice said in a whisper from the other end.

"Who is this?" Shane asked.

"I thought if I just went somewhere big, it'd be better!"

There was panic to the delivery, the whispered words tumbling out in a rush as the person on the other end spoke. Something tickled the back of Shane's mind. There was a familiarity there, something he recognized. But he couldn't place his finger on it.

"I think it's going to kill me."

"Who is this?" Shane repeated.

"Shane," the voice said, even more quietly now. "Shane Ryan?"

"Yeah," he replied. "You called me, so why don't you let me know who you are."

"Big Bear said you were a good man. He feared you, though. I could tell. He was grateful but scared."

"Big Bear?" Shane said.

He had met a man named Big Bear on a trip to Canada when he was dealing with the Iron Tournament and a powerful ghost named Lazarus. Big Bear worked in a bar. He could see ghosts, sense them even, but he was terrified of his power. His cousin had become possessed and walked from Canada to Shane's house before setting up shop in the cellar.

"Martin, is that you?"

Martin Marner was Big Bear's cousin, a blacksmith in a speck of a town in the middle of nowhere. He'd helped Shane forge some weapons to fight Lazarus before Martin became possessed. Shane had saved him, but Martin wasn't in the best headspace when Big Bear took him back to Canada. Not that any normal person would be.

"It's killed so many people."

"Martin, what the hell are you talking about?" Shane demanded.

He heard the other man sniffle and gasp. He was sobbing over the phone, but trying to hold it back.

"I left home. I had to get somewhere… loud. Somewhere big. I thought Boston would be good. It never sleeps, it's never quiet here, and I would be close to my aunt Hannah."

"Okay, that's great," Shane said.

"But I found out she'd died months ago, and I had nowhere to go and I ended up… it's like it was before. It's dark and cold and there's something down here with us. Like before. Like in your cellar."

Shane held the cigarette a short distance from his lips and then lowered his hand.

"Where are you, Martin?"

"In the tunnels. In the old tunnels. I think no one's supposed to be here. It doesn't want me to be here."

## Chapter 2
# What Waits

"You're going to need to start making some sense, Martin," Shane told him.

Martin went off on more than one tangent about losing work, getting lost, being in tunnels, and something in the darkness. The desperation in his voice was clear, but he was also borderline incoherent.

Shane had not spent a lot of time with Martin when they met, but Martin had not been like this before. He was a skilled artist, and he seemed on the ball back home. After what happened with Lazarus, it was hard to say. Big Bear hadn't contacted Shane again, and that was fine. But on the phone just now, Martin sounded like he needed professional help beyond anything Shane could offer.

"Please, we just… I just need you to come here."

"Where?" Shane asked. "Where are you in Boston?"

"I… it's called Tremont? It's the tunnels. We're in the tunnels. I'm trying to keep hidden, but I think it can see everything in the dark."

"Alright, just keep doing what you're doing to stay safe, okay? I'll find you. What's the number you're calling from?"

There was another sob on the line, a gasp of air, and the phone went dead. Shane stared at it for a moment, waiting to see if Martin would call back. He did not.

"Martin from the cellar?" Carl asked. Shane nodded.

"He said he's in Boston. Thinks something is after him, but he sounds squirrelly. Not sure he's in his right mind."

"After what happened, he could have suffered some long-term problems," Carl suggested.

"Was thinking the same. But he sounds adamant that something is after him. Something in the subway, I think."

"Hmm."

Carl looked like he was mulling over the proposition.

"Boston has the oldest subway in America, does it not? More than enough time for some ghosts to have called it home."

"The subway runs under most of the city. Any ghost could get in there; it's not that deep. He said Tremont, though."

"Are you familiar?" Carl asked.

"I've heard of it. Should be easy enough to find."

Carl stood up and turned to face Shane as he stood as well.

"Then you are leaving?"

"Yeah, I have to. I feel partially responsible for—" Shane replied.

His friend nodded.

"Good. You have done little since we returned. It's good to get out. Fresh air, as they say."

"Boston subways aren't known for their freshness."

"Even so," Carl said. "I will be fine here. We all will."

"I know."

After their return, Shane made a few changes around the house. If Coulson returned, none of them would matter; he was a special case and nothing Shane could reasonably plan for. But he had moved the haunted items around, placing them in more secure locations. If anyone from the Endless Night had previously learned the house's layout, they would be in the dark once again.

The ghosts knew of the danger the Endless Night presented. Shane had established a protocol for hiding or fighting, but that was easier said than done. Eloise, in particular, was unpredictable and not known to listen to instructions all the time. If someone broke in, she was just as likely to tear off their face as remain hidden in the shadows.

Shane was as confident as he could be, though. He had been confident before Coulson had arrived. That someone would invade his home and take Carl away was not even a thing he'd considered. But if Coulson had taught Shane nothing else, it was that he didn't know everything, nor could he. Some things were impossible to prepare for. All he could do is be as ready as he possibly could.

Carl was right. Shane had not been out of the house much since they had returned from down south. He'd gone out for cigarettes and food and the odd walk through the neighborhood; that was it.

But going to Boston to potentially save a man he barely knew from what might have been a ghost in the subway was not the way Shane wanted to get out on the road. On the other hand, he didn't have a preferred plan of action. It wasn't like he was hoping to be invited to someone's wedding, or that he wanted to head out for a fishing weekend. He wasn't sure what he wanted, or if he wanted anything at all.

There was something relaxing about the time he'd spent after returning from Florida, but there was an underlying anxiety, too. Not doing anything was becoming as stressful as being thrust into situations against his will. Maybe he was just the kind of person who couldn't find happiness anymore. Hell, maybe he only felt alive when someone was trying to kill him.

Shane drove the familiar route down to Boston, leaving soon after his call with Martin ended. Carl would explain what was happening to the others, all of whom had been on edge since Shane's return. It would take time for everyone to settle down again. They were all dead anyway, so they had a lot less to worry about than Shane did.

Tremont Street cut through a major part of Boston's downtown and extended south, though Shane couldn't remember how far it went. He was certain he'd traveled the road many times in the past, but he'd not put a lot of effort into remembering the details of where it went.

Going to Boston had never been one of Shane's favorite activities. Going to downtown Boston even less so. Unfortunately, the Tremont line was in one of the busiest parts of town. He wasn't sure how many of the old tunnels were still in use, but he knew many of them were in the heart of downtown. That meant being around people and potentially drawing unwanted attention. It was not easy to deal with a ghost in front of a crowd.

Shane parked in front of an AMC theater and crossed the street to Boston Common. The only thing he remembered for sure about the Tremont line was that there was a station somewhere near Boylston and another near Park. That information was vague enough to be utterly useless.

There were well over one hundred active subway stations in Boston. Shane had made little use of them and couldn't guess his best option to find Martin or a subway ghost.

If Martin was living in abandoned tunnels, then they had to be the century-old ones that were sealed up in the 1940s. Access to those would have been hidden from the public: There was no way the local government would invite people to wander around in ancient death traps. Finding Martin's location would take some time.

Boston Common was the oldest public park in the country. Dating back to some time in the 1600s, it had seen more than its share of death over the years. The park was home to more ghosts than most public parks Shane had encountered. On a long enough timeline, more deaths were going to tally up in one spot; it was unavoidable.

A ghost could probably point him in the right direction, but he'd need to find one alone around the subway that he could talk to without looking suspicious or crazy. That was easier said than done in Boston Common. He could see hundreds of people as he crossed Tremont from the theater.

The weather was nice, and that attracted a good number of the living to the park. People walking dogs, riding bikes, and eating lunch by the frog pond. The number of ghosts was lower than what Shane had expected but still high. He could see a few dozen just from the outskirts, several looking like they'd time-traveled to the park from the Revolutionary War and others clearly from the 1800s.

Shane scouted the park looking for ones that returned eye contact or looked like the sort with a need for conversation. There was an air of desperation around some ghosts that flagged them as potential sources of information. Ones that loomed around the living, reading phones and books over people's shoulders were often good bets. Better than the loners who looked like they were trying to avoid the living.

He approached the bandstand, watching the handful of pedestrians and cyclists and the reactions of the few ghosts that were out and about. His eyes drifted to the nearest bench, where an old man in a ball cap was reading a magazine while the ghost of a man in his early twenties who was dressed in a pair of oily blue coveralls read over his shoulder.

Shane watched the ghost smile and nod, his lips moving slightly as he read whatever the old man was reading. When the man turned the page too soon, the ghost frowned and reached out as though planning to turn the page back, then stopped himself.

*Perfect*, Shane thought. He was probably the most bored ghost in the whole park.

He approached the bench and had a seat next to the old man, closer than was appropriate. He wasn't touching the man, but he was in his personal space.

The man looked up from his magazine and made eye contact with Shane, who stared at him.

"Can I help you?" the man asked. He was in his late sixties if Shane had to guess, and his thick glasses made his eyes look too large.

"No," Shane replied.

The ghost frowned, looking at Shane.

"Do you mind?" the old man said.

"No," Shane said again.

They had reached a social stalemate in fewer than ten words. Shane was violating the man's personal space and refused to correct it. By the rules of polite society, there was little left for the man to do.

With a grunt of dissatisfaction, the old man gathered a soft-sided briefcase and his magazine, got to his feet, and left.

"Geez, man," the ghost muttered, watching him go. "What the heck?"

"It was a boring magazine anyway," Shane replied. "History of billiards? Come on."

The ghost locked eyes with Shane, that surprised look he'd seen more than a few times crossing the spirit's face.

"You can see me?" the ghost asked.

"Yeah. Have a seat," Shane offered, nodding to the spot the magazine man had vacated.

The spirit circled the bench quickly, now visibly excited, and sat. He was younger than Shane had thought at first, maybe only in his late teens. He was dressed like a mechanic and his flesh was less naturally pale than it seemed ashen, like he had been covered in dried mud. His left eye moved slower than his right, and he was missing a few teeth but otherwise seemed unmarred.

"I'm Jaker. I never met no one who could see me before. This is great!"

"Never? How long have you been in the park, Jaker?"

"Oh, heck, I don't know. What year is it? I drowned in the river in 1987."

"Been a few years," Shane said.

"You're telling me. You seen what they got these days? Phones that have TVs and computers in them and all kinds of stuff. It's gnarly. Hey, what's your name?"

"Shane," he answered.

Jaker wiped his hand on his coveralls and held it out. Shane shrugged and took it, the cold of the ghostly flesh uncomfortable in his grip as they shook.

"Wow!" Jaker said, grinning wide enough to show off three gaps in his teeth. "This is great. Can you see all the ghosts or just me? Oh, did you come here looking for me? Did my ma send you?"

"She didn't. I need a favor if you're up for it," Shane answered.

"Mister, I've been reading half magazine articles and single book chapters in this park for years. I'm up for anything," Jaker replied eagerly.

"Good. I need a guide to get me into the subway."

Jaker looked at him with a perplexed expression then pointed somewhere vaguely to the north.

"There's a station right on Park Street if you need the subway."

Shane shook his head.

"I need the subway no one's supposed to be in."

## Chapter 3
## What Lies Beneath

Jaker led Shane down into the Park Street station, talking the entire time about how he drowned in the river one night after chasing some thieves away from the oil change place where he'd worked. It was a story full of tangents and much of it was lost in the sounds of the city. The ghost was unaware that Shane could barely hear him, but he kept walking the entire time and that was all Shane needed.

The Park Street station was near the corner of Park and Tremont at the edge of Boston Common. It was as busy as any station Shane had been to and definitely not where he was going to find Martin, but Jaker assured him it was where he wanted to be.

Shane kept quiet while the ghost droned on, not wanting to look suspicious in front of commuters.

Jaker ignored everyone and passed the crowd of people waiting for the next train to roll through, heading toward the end of the platform while Shane followed casually behind. The ghost reached the end and jumped down onto the tracks, continuing south down the tunnel. Shane stopped at the edge and said nothing. There were at least two dozen people on the platform, including a transit cop. He would not jump into the tunnel in front of everyone.

Jaker kept talking as he wandered farther and farther away. Shane cleared his throat and pretended to read his phone. He started whistling after a moment, glancing from the phone to the platform to the tunnel and back.

No one was paying him any mind, but Jaker had nearly vanished around a curve in the tunnel. He finally looked back and saw that Shane had not followed him.

"Hey!" the ghost yelled, waving. Shane stared at him in silence. "Hey Shane, you gotta come this way!"

Shane remained still and silent until something seemed to click and Jaker walked back.

"Oh, geez, you can't just jump down here, can you?" the ghost asked when he returned to the platform.

"Not if I want to get very far," Shane said.

"That makes sense. So, what do we do now? If you want an abandoned tunnel, you have to go that way," Jaker said, pointing back to where he had been.

"Normally, I'd wait until things cleared up, but this is the middle of the day in downtown Boston. I'm going to need a distraction."

"Okay," Jaker said, nodding and smiling.

Shane sighed.

"I need you to make a distraction."

"Oh!" Jaker said, grinning. "You want me to make a scene?"

"Just be loud. And over there," Shane answered, nodding to the far side of the platform.

Jaker giggled like a child and made off without another word. He brushed past people waiting for the train, causing them to feel uncomfortable as the burst of mysterious cold ran across their bodies, until he reached the farthest edge of the platform near the entrance.

The ghost offered Shane a thumbs-up and then jumped, swatting the overhead lights like he was King Kong batting a plane from the sky.

Fluorescent bulbs exploded, and the fixture swung and creaked as glass rained down from the ceiling. People nearby screamed and ran while everyone's attention was suddenly pulled toward what just happened.

With a fully attentive audience who could not see him, Jaker leaped again and smashed the next light.

Some commuters panicked and made a break for the exit while others backed away, eyes up and wary of what might break next. Shane ducked down off the platform and stuck to the wall of the tunnel, running down the way Jaker had shown him and heading out of sight of those at the platform.

Shane ran until he could no longer see the platform around the curve in the tunnel. He slowed his pace and waited until Jaker could catch up with him. From where he stood, there were no obvious options to go except straight forward. The tunnel had no access points that he could see and nothing of note beyond some switching equipment, the odd bit of trash, and lights recessed into the walls.

When Jaker caught up, he was still grinning like a fool and shouted his enthusiasm with a loud cheer. Shane was tempted to tell him to keep it down, but it wasn't as though anyone would hear the ghost.

"That was fun. This has been the best time I've had since I died. Which is kind of sad, I suppose."

"Some ghosts spend centuries trapped in boxes," Shane replied. Jaker didn't have it so bad, all things being equal.

"For real? How does a ghost get trapped in a box?"

"Don't worry about it. You know anything about ghosts that hang out down here?"

Jaker shrugged.

"Not a lot. I like being in the sun, so I don't come down here much. I know a few of them stay here. Some folks who'd died on the tracks, or in the tunnels. They're real old, you know."

"That's what I heard," Shane said. "What about violent ghosts? Anyone like that down here?"

Jaker's eyes narrowed.

"You one of them Haunted Boston people? Looking for spooky

things for a magazine or… the internet?"

"Not exactly. Just looking for a friend who might be lost down here."

"Oh." Jaker nodded. "There's a lot of old tunnels covered up. Some of them the city doesn't even know about anymore."

"Who does know?"

"I like to stay in the sun. I know sometimes other ghosts talk about it down here. There's street people down here in some places, but I don't know much about them. They don't read much and even when they do, it's usually old things. I like reading new magazines or the internet. I like funny lists. You ever read those?"

"No," Shane said. "Was that a yes about the violent ghosts, or no?"

"Maybe?" Jaker answered after a moment. "I know people go missing. Not just dying down here, but missing. I hear people talk sometimes. There's a story about a boogeyman in the tunnels. I don't believe in any boogeyman, but then I thought, heck, I'm a ghost. People might think I'm the boogeyman. Especially if I was dragging them down dark tunnels."

"They might think that," Shane agreed.

"But I haven't heard anyone talk about that in a while."

Jaker was not as helpful as Shane would have hoped. But at least he got him into the tunnels, and that was something.

"Right there is what you're looking for," the ghost said. They had to be halfway to the next station when he stopped to point out an old, rusty door set into the wall.

"Where does that go?" Shane asked.

"It's not supposed to go anywhere, it's all locked up. But I was down here maybe five years after I drowned and saw a few people pick the lock and sneak through to a tunnel I never saw when I was alive. Part of the old line they replaced with the one we're on now."

"And people live in there?"

Jaker approached the door and shrugged again.

"Like I said, I'm not down here so much. But they were going in there for something, and if your friend lives down here, it's probably in the tunnels the police don't go to, right?"

"Right," Shane agreed.

He inspected the lock and saw that it was not as old as the door in which it was fixed. Someone had replaced it within the last few years. Picking locks was a skill he'd had to rely on once or twice in the past, but this one looked complicated.

"How'd they pick this?"

Jaker leaned in for a closer look.

"Oh, no, it wasn't this lock. It was like an old-time lock before. This one is probably to keep people like you out."

"Well, it's working."

"You're lucky you brought me then," the ghost replied. He vanished into the wall of the tunnel without another word. Shane waited outside the door as a low rumble began in the distance. Then one of the lights set into the wall flickered.

The door remained still and silent. The rumbling was faint but growing louder. Shane looked down at the track, estimating the distance between it and the door at which he was waiting. The space was narrow, more than enough room for a man to stand and be safely away from the rail. But what if a train passed?

His mind raced back to the last time he'd been in a subway tunnel in Boston. Had he paid any attention to the clearance between the car and the wall? Of course not. Why would anyone?

Another light flickered, and he heard the horn of a train in the distance. The rumbling grew louder.

"How's that door coming, Jaker?" he asked. There was no answer from the ghost on the other side.

"Jaker!"

Shane pounded his fist against the door twice.

"There's no knob," came the ghost's muffled reply.

"What?"

"It's a key lock on this side, too. It's not just a knob you unlock."

The sound was distinct now, the repetitive, staccato rumbling of steel wheels on a steel track. It was approaching. And it was fast.

"Jaker, I don't have a lot of time out here."

"What should I do?" the ghost asked.

"Open the damn door!"

"How?"

The horn of the train blared again. Shane could feel the vibrations in his feet. Lights on both walls flickered and even the wall shook and hummed with the power of the approaching engine.

"Break it! I don't care, just open it!"

Jaker didn't reply. Shane pounded on the door as the train thundered ever forward. The track continued on a curve so he could not see how far away it was. He had only the sound and vibrations as his guide.

He slammed his shoulder into the metal door and grunted. The lock held firm, barely even a rattle. He pushed his full weight against it again and again. Too much time had passed since he realized the train was coming, there was no way he could make it back to the platform. He had a minute if he was lucky.

"Jaker!" Shane yelled, the sound of his voice swallowed by the train's cacophony. He grabbed the door handle and hissed, the metal freezing his flesh.

"Hit it again," the ghost yelled from inside. A light spread across the wall of the tunnel ahead, right at the curve. The headlights of the subway came into view as it roared and rattled toward him.

Gritting his teeth, Shane slammed his body as hard as he could against the door just as the headlights of the train rounded the bend, blinding him in the process.

Something metallic snapped, and the door shook but stayed

closed. Jaker yelled something Shane couldn't hear over the train and forced his shoulder into the door one last time as the train barreled toward him.

The door fell open awkwardly, the rusty hinges squealing like a wounded animal. He fell forward and onto the floor as the train rushed past, the air in its wake sucking the cooler, stale air from the room around Shane like a vacuum.

He rolled over and kicked his feet, pushing away from the door just to be safe as car after car rolled by, a symphony of steel that threatened to deafen him at such close range.

"Jesus, would you look at that?" Jaker said, standing over Shane. "You would have been pancaked if you waited another minute."

"If I waited?" Shane said from the floor before getting to his feet. Jaker shrugged awkwardly.

"You got me stressed out, I wasn't sure what to do."

"What did you do?" Shane asked, looking at the door. The lock had been torn out of it, chunks of metal broken off around the latch.

"Figured the lock was new, but the door was old and fragile. Just got it a bit cold," the ghost said, holding up his hand.

Shane grunted, impressed by the ghost's ingenuity. He looked around the room as the train's brakes squealed in the distance.

"Now, where are we?"

## Chapter 4
# No Man's Land

There were no lights beyond the door. Shane pulled out his Zippo and lit it, exposing a small, sparse room. It looked like there had once been equipment within, based on a discolored spot on the wall and capped wires. Now, there was just scrap metal and a pair of rusted-out old lockers on the far wall next to another door.

Shane approached. It was in much worse condition than the first and no one had bothered to replace the lock. He turned the handle, and it moved slowly, rust flaking off on his hands before the stiff, corroded hinges finally gave way under his efforts.

Cold air rushed toward Shane, stale, and unpleasant. The flame from the lighter flickered before settling down once more. Beyond was a new tunnel. It was as black as night, and only a few feet ahead was visible in the faint light of the Zippo.

"Do you know where we are?" Shane asked.

"A tunnel," Jaker offered unhelpfully. Shane held the lighter high, looking in both directions.

*We could be headed south. Tremont goes a little farther north before it has to turn lest it hit the river*, Shane thought. He was trying to keep a rough idea of directions in his head, but the subway didn't follow the street maps from above, which made judging distances and directions hard, especially in tunnels that had been sealed off and unused for ages.

"Is this even Tremont anymore?"

He could see no signs on the walls in the new tunnel. The walls were covered in ancient tiles that had grayed or yellowed with age depending on how damp they were.

"I honestly have no idea," Jaker replied. The ghost seemed on edge now, looking up and down the tunnel like he was spooked by the idea of being there.

"See anything down there?" Shane asked, holding the lighter higher.

"A tunnel," the ghost said again.

Shane sighed and started walking. Wherever he was, he was at least near Tremont, where Martin had said his location was. Even if the young man was gone, if there were others around, someone would have to know him.

"How come you can see ghosts?" Jaker asked as they walked, his version of small talk.

"Just something I can do," Shane answered.

"You ever get scared?"

"Of ghosts?"

"Yeah. Ghosts are scary, right? That's what I always thought when I was a kid," Jaker explained.

"Do you scare yourself?"

"You know what I mean. Some ghosts are bad news."

"Yeah, some are," Shane agreed.

The air shifted now and then as they walked. The Zippo struggled to stay lit, and Shane scanned the tunnel as far as the light allowed, but there was still nothing to see. The only sounds were muffled and distant, things like trains in other tunnels. Sometimes, they passed grates and pipes that allowed the faint sounds of the city above to filter down. No voices, though, no footsteps or signs of movement. Not even a rat.

Shane paused in the center of the tunnel, looking behind them and then forward. They had traveled far enough that they had rounded another curve and even with proper lighting, he wouldn't have been able to see the door through which they'd entered.

"What?" Jaker whispered, looking back as well.

"There's no rats in here," Shane pointed out. The ghost looked at him.

"Isn't that a good thing?"

"It's a ghost thing. When's the last time you saw a rat near you?"

Jaker looked thoughtful for a moment, considering Shane's question.

"Most animals don't like to hang around ghosts," Shane clarified, moving on once more.

The air was chilly, but it was an abandoned subway tunnel, so there was no reason to expect it to be warm. It could have indicated the presence of a ghost, but not necessarily.

"I don't see anyone," Jaker said.

"Me neither. Just keep your eyes open."

"I don't even need to blink anymore," the ghost pointed out.

Shane looked down. The train tracks beneath them looked old. The metal was orange with rust and in some places, joints had warped and left gaps between rails. Any train that traveled the tracks these days would derail instantly.

Trash was the only truly out-of-place thing Shane could see in the tunnel. There were cans and wrappers here and there. Some could have been as old as the tunnel, but others were clearly new. A plastic Pepsi bottle full of yellow fluid rested against a wall. Some pallets were stacked nearby and strewn with mildewed and motheaten sheets.

They paused to pick through the ramshackle encampment. There was evidence of a fire, but it could have been years old. Only chunks of charcoal and burnt wood, rusted food cans, and scraps of fabric and plastic remained.

"I don't think anyone's been here in a while," Jaker suggested. Shane nodded, kicking around some piles of junk and finding nothing of interest.

They continued deeper into the tunnel, the sounds of distant trains sometimes getting close enough to rattle the walls and shake loose dust from above them.

It was unclear how far they'd traveled when Jaker came to a stop, standing in the middle of the track. Shane had walked several steps before he realized the ghost was no longer beside him.

"Jaker?" Shane turned back.

The ghost's expression was one of disappointment.

"I've got some bad news," he whispered.

"End of the line?" Shane asked.

Jaker looked confused for a moment and Shane nodded to his feet.

"You can't go any farther."

"Oh. Well, yeah. I'm too far from the river. Boston Common is already pretty far for me, but it's the nicest place I can go. I didn't think we'd be this far from—"

"It's fine." Shane replied.

The ghost was upset, but it was not something either of them could control.

"I can wait here if you want."

"I don't know if I'll be back this way. I appreciate your help, though," Shane told him.

The ghost nodded, pacing awkwardly for a moment.

"Alright. But listen, when you're done, do you want to come back to the park? Just to let me know if it all worked out," he said.

"Yeah, I can swing back. Don't worry, I don't plan on dying down here or anything."

"Bet everyone thinks that," the ghost replied.

Shane laughed.

"Head back to the park. I'll see you when I finish up."

"Are you sure you're going to be okay?" Jaker asked.

Shane wondered what the ghost's plan might be if he answered, "No." It wasn't like the ghost could call anyone or make plans to help.

"I'm good. Thank you for your help," Shane said.

He turned from the ghost and kept on his way deeper into the darkness. The next time he looked back, Jaker was gone.

Alone in the tunnel, Shane was more aware of every sound, and the absence of sound, as he made his way south. The trash piles became more frequent the deeper he traveled, some of them graduating to full campsites with old tents or cardboard structures assembled with ropes and support posts.

None of the impromptu camps looked recent, though, and they were certainly no longer inhabited. The few things Shane could find to date the structures, old newspapers or magazines, were at least two years old.

Shane had just lifted a tarp propped up by boxes and a two-by-four, inspecting the contents within, when a flash of movement just beyond the edge of the Zippo's light drew his attention.

A pair of spirits stood shoulder to shoulder, a man and a woman. Neither had eyes that Shane could see, and both had the same gaunt, sunken features as though they had starved for a long time before death had taken them. They wore a mishmash of clothing, layers upon layers, and the male's laceless shoes looked a few sizes too large for his slender frame.

They watched him dig through the empty camps, unaware that he could see them. Neither made a move toward him nor seemed to have any threatening intent, but Shane knew how quickly those tides could shift.

"Not wrecking your home here, am I?" he asked, standing up and leaving the tent half collapsed. The female ghost took a step back, surprised, while the male narrowed his empty eye sockets.

"You shouldn't be here," the male ghost said. His voice was barely more than a whisper, low and distant.

"Just passing through," Shane explained. "You wouldn't happen to know a guy named Martin, would you?"

"You shouldn't be here." The woman's voice was louder, clearer than the man's, with a hint of anger.

"Got that part. I'm just looking for someone who said he's been staying down here in the Tremont tunnels."

"Why?" the man asked.

Shane rummaged through some of the refuse in the camp, seeing a familiar shape under some discarded food wrappers. He pulled out a cheap looking dollar store flashlight and pressed the button. The bulb came to life, dim and yellow, providing barely any illumination.

The light only made the smallest spot visible, and the ghosts retreated into the shadows. He could no longer see them.

"Got a tip that someone needed a hand getting out of here," Shane called out.

He waited, still like a statue, and felt the air currents around him shift. Cool air brushed against his face, but it was gentle. The male ghost appeared within the glow of the flashlight, not rushing to attack, just drifting into view.

"No one here," the ghost said. "You want to go south."

"I was going south," Shane pointed out. The ghost shook his head and pointed into the dark.

"The tunnel ends ahead. Walled off. You need to be on the other side."

"He doesn't need to know anything," the female ghost said. She was still hidden in the shadows, and her voice seemed to come from everywhere at once.

"He's just looking for someone," her partner whispered.

"He doesn't belong here."

"Nothing belongs here," the male countered.

"How do I get to the other side?" Shane asked.

The female ghost's face appeared from the darkness. The empty eyes were directed at Shane, seeing without seeing.

"Go back the way you came. The people down here are all just waiting to die."

"That a fact?" Shane asked. "You two wouldn't be helping them along, would you?"

"Leave now and—"

The female ghost's words were cut off as Shane took her by the throat. She gasped, surprised by the unexpected move. Shane pulled the ghost closer.

"We can keep this civil. You tell me how to get where I want to go, and then I go there and leave you alone. You start making me suspicious that you're the ones down here making people disappear, and maybe I have to do something about it."

Shane didn't think the pair were the ghosts Martin had talked about. Nothing more than a gut feeling, but neither came across as menacing. Even before they knew Shane could see them, they held back as if hiding. Their first concern was to keep him away. They were loners, inhospitable maybe, but they didn't strike him as killers.

"We never hurt anyone," the dead man said, taking Shane's arm and trying to pull it from his partner. His grip held, even as the ghost's froze his arm.

Shane relented, letting the other ghost loose and pulling free of the male ghost's grip.

"What do you know about the ghost that hurts people down here?" he asked.

A silent look passed between the spirits, and Shane held the flashlight higher to better illuminate them all.

"We just want to be left alone," the woman said.

The other ghost nodded.

"Keep to ourselves, that's what we do. We never wanted trouble."

"Not what I asked," Shane said.

"He stays on that side mostly," the male said at last. His partner looked unhappy but didn't voice any further opposition. "Around where the homeless live."

"Who is *he*?"

The female ghost shook her head.

"Don't know and don't want to. He's trouble. That's why we keep to ourselves."

"What do you care? You're dead already."

"Doesn't mean much," the male replied. "He's strong. He can hurt ghosts; I've seen him do it."

"Is he the one that killed you?"

The male sighed, and the female just kept shaking her head.

"What does it matter? We stay here. We keep to ourselves. He doesn't come around here much 'cause it's empty now. Been empty for years."

"Just tell me how to get to the other side, and I'll leave you to it," Shane said.

"Are you one of them?" the male asked, looking at Shane then his companion. She grimaced and looked at Shane.

"He killed all the others. He'll kill you, too."

## Chapter 5
## The Forgotten

Reluctant though they might have been, the ghosts led Shane to the end of the line and the bricked-up tunnel that sealed the living part of Boston's underground.

"There's a station just a stone's throw from this wall. The tunnel curves around us to the left. You want to go that way," the male ghost said, pointing to an empty platform at Shane's right. It was covered in broken tiles and more ragged, forgotten campsites made of junk. At one time, there must have been dozens of people living there.

"How many people have come looking for this ghost?" Shane asked. The two ghosts assumed he was part of some ghost-hunting group, but no one had succeeded in their hunt so far.

"A dozen?" the male said. The female nodded.

"Maybe more. Not so many these days. But they used to come often. Groups of them, and one would venture in to find Switchyard while the others waited and monitored. Once the screaming stopped, the others usually left."

"Switchyard?" Shane asked. The male shrugged.

"We started calling him that. He's always in the empty train tunnels."

"Where does he call home?"

The female ghost shook her head.

"In the dark somewhere. We don't go looking."

"But he comes after the people who live down here?"

"Now and then. There's no sense to it. No reason. Never even heard him speak before. He might take two in a day, then no one for months. It's like he gets this rage and needs to take it out on whoever he can," the male explained.

"What does he do with the bodies?"

The ghosts shared a glance.

"Never been a body that I've seen," the male said. "Not like anyone ever comes looking. Until you, I guess."

"Until me."

He hoped that didn't mean Martin would be a body when he found him. Whoever or whatever Switchyard was, he sounded like a sadist. A ghost that took joy in hurting others and gave into his whims whenever they arose. If there was no set pattern or timing, then he probably ran on instinct and emotion. He would be unpredictable.

"Is there anything else you can tell me about Switchyard? Places he's seen most often, routines he has, anything like that?"

"No," the female ghost replied. "He's not like that. He doesn't go for walks. He doesn't talk. He doesn't do anything. He's like a predator. He comes out to hunt."

"When did he start?" Shane asked, hoping for some kind of inside edge. The female ghost just shook her head again.

"No idea."

Shane climbed onto the platform, dusted off his hands, and headed toward a hole someone had smashed into the far wall. The tile and bricks were pushed haphazardly to one side, and beyond was more darkness.

"That will take you down to the south tunnel end. There's a connection to the storm sewers back there; that's how most people get in from street level. Makes it easy for the ones who live there. Also gives the only light you'll find down here. Just keep straight. If you take any of the branches, you'll get lost. Or worse," the female spirit explained.

Shane held the light toward the hole, illuminating nothing but a pile of rubble on the far side.

"Where—" Shane began, looking back.

The ghosts had vanished, leaving him alone. The platform was like a grave, cold and silent. He grunted and ducked through the opening to the southern tunnel beyond.

The new tunnel was wider and looked older from what Shane could see. The brickwork brought to mind something that should have predated subways.

He pulled a cigarette from his pack and placed it in his mouth and used his Zippo to light it. The flashlight barely emitted light now and was mostly just a faint, yellow spot. The batteries must have been nearly dead and shaking it no longer worked to give it any kind of boost.

Despite the ghost telling him light came from somewhere ahead, Shane saw nothing. Behind him, the tunnel had been walled up with the same brick and some metal bumpers that looked like they prevented trains from driving into the wall. He wondered how fast a train would need to go to burst through such a thing.

Shane headed further south. This new tunnel was quieter. The rumble of distant trains still penetrated the darkness, but it was softer here. The walls shook less, and the echo was more muffled. Even the air was different. Cold, but still. There was barely a hint of movement to it, and the flashlight's yellow beam flickered.

He had walked for no more than ten minutes when he noticed more stray bricks in his path. There were one or two small pieces at first, but then more and more. Fragments became halves became whole bricks mixed with stones and dirt.

Shane shook the flashlight, trying to drum up enough juice from the batteries to widen the circle of light as he held it high. The path ahead of him ended but not in a wall that had been built intentionally like the one on the other end.

The ceiling had crumbled at some point, and tons of brick had been dumped onto the old track, sealing off the rest of the tunnel. Shane waved the light from one side to another. There was no break anywhere; the coverage was wall to wall. He looked up to the ceiling.

The pile of brick and dirt rose on a sharp slope to the ceiling. The size at the base was more than twice as wide as where the ceiling had caved in. Shane had no doubt the wall would be impossible to dig through. Even if he tried, he probably would have released more from above. It was impassable.

To the right, only a yard back from the edge of the collapse, a passageway branched right. Not a subway tunnel, but a walking path, connecting a platform to something lost in the darkness.

The spacing seemed too intentional to Shane. A collapse at the end of a platform, right next to a new passage into the dark. It looked like someone didn't want people traveling the tunnel south. Or maybe they didn't want anyone going north from the other side. It left him with two choices: He could return the way he'd come or take the mystery path, even though the ghosts had told him not to leave the tunnel, and not to take any of the branches.

Smoke from his cigarette drifted before Shane's eyes, and he squinted in the darkness. No sound, no airflow, nothing came from the passage on the right. He climbed up to the platform and stood at the passage mouth, holding the light in as far as he could. More ancient brick, and the remnants of a sign that was mostly worn down to nothing. He could see an arrow pointing the way he faced and maybe the word "station", but the rest was gone.

*Everything leads somewhere*, he thought.

The light dimmed even more, flickering and flashing in the confined space, which was only wide enough for two people abreast. Subway travelers must have been a more tolerant lot a century ago.

When Shane emerged on the other side, he did not know where he was. Every tunnel, and the passage as well, curved slightly this way or that. He felt like he might have been under Boston Common. He might have passed it altogether as well. There was no way to know.

The next station platform was as old as the one he'd just left. But there were no ramshackle camps here and no sign anyone had lived in the space. Dust was thick on the floor, and Shane left distinct footprints. Around him, he could see the remains of older travelers, but even those prints were filled with thin dust layers. It had to have been years since anyone stood where he did. Anyone living, at least.

The adjacent subway tunnel looked to extend both north and south, but Shane stuck with the southern track, hoping to find wherever Martin had ended up. At some point, the tunnels had to lead him to people, or a way out so he could reorient himself. Even if he didn't find what he needed, the ghosts had told him there was an outside way to reach Tremont through storm sewers. He'd find what he needed soon enough.

Shane jumped from the platform and headed down the tunnel. The sound of distant trains was now so quiet, it was only something he noticed if he stopped and listened. The ambient sound was a strange hum of a still room mixed with the sound of his footsteps.

His feet crunched on dry, old wood and detritus from a century of darkness and obscurity. The cool air was dead still. He kept his pace brisk but still slow enough to be cautious. He didn't want to run into anything with his dim light, or trip over any unseen obstacles.

Then Shane stopped thirty paces from the platform. The flashlight flickered slightly, but it was still enough to illuminate a dark spot on the tunnel wall. He moved the light closer and leaned in. A stain on the wall in the shape of a hand drew his attention.

The light wavered and made it look like it was moving. Shane leaned in closer and touched the handprint with his finger. Old, black flakes of dried blood fell away. He lowered the light to just above the ground. The stone and the edge of the old track were bathed in it; old blood dried to a dark film. It was ancient, he couldn't say how old exactly, but he guessed the climate of the tunnel had preserved it well enough to keep it intact.

No insects or rats had fed on it. Blood had spilled and remained there untainted. Pints of it, from the size of the stain. Enough that whoever had lost it surely hadn't survived. But there was no body, no flesh or bone anywhere. Just the puddle and the handprint.

Shane lifted the flashlight and looked up and down the tunnel wall as far as he could see. No other splatters or stains. No sign of any additional struggle.

He finished the cigarette and pinched out the ember, fieldstripping the butt before reaching for a replacement. No sooner had he lifted it to his lips when a burst of cold swept over him from behind. The faint light of the flashlight flickered and died, fading to a brief afterglow before going totally black.

Shane stood still in the darkness and frowned, putting the cigarette back in its pack. He tossed the light to the ground. The glass broke and scattered in the old blood stain. The cold air remained in place, like a physical thing. Shane could not see the ghost, could not tell if it was in front of or behind him, but it was there.

"Not the friendliest entrance," he said out loud. There was no guarantee it was Switchyard; there were probably many ghosts in the tunnel. Jaker had said as much.

No one answered. He stared into the darkness, part of his mind waiting for his eyes to adjust while another part recognized they never would. There was nothing to adjust to, and no faint light to aid in seeing. He would work blind.

Something clicked a few paces ahead. A quick, barely noticeable sound. Under normal circumstances, Shane would have paid it no attention. But in the dark, it was the only sound.

*Click.*

It was soft. Something thick and solid tapping against something hard and metallic, like a knife tapping a wall, maybe. Or a nail on a subway track.

*Click.*

Shane stood his ground. The sound was close.

*Click.*

It had moved, but barely. Circling his position to the left.

*Click.*

The sound came from the other side now. Shane turned and a cool current drifted over the light, giving it a hint of life. It cast just enough light to illuminate the nearly white hand lined with thick, purple veins that held it aloft.

## Chapter 6
# The Cold Hands of Death

Shane fell back as the flashlight swung through the air, nearly hitting him in the face. The ghost flung the cheap plastic across the tunnel before setting upon him in the darkness, and he could feel the weight of something kneeling on his stomach. Hands like ice came for Shane's throat.

He had seen just enough in the dim light. Nails gray and cracked and curved like the talons of a bird. Flesh as pale as milk, stained with purple lividity marks and thick, squirming veins.

Shane's hands were up defensively. He caught the ghost's wrists and held firm, then rolled quickly to the left. The spirit, not knowing Shane could lay hands on it, was not prepared for the counter. It flopped over quickly, allowing Shane to switch their positions so he was on top of the ghost.

It writhed and bucked in his grip. With the ghost's wrists held firmly in his fists, Shane punched down. He hit something soft, maybe the face or upper chest, he wasn't sure.

It struggled harder in Shane's grasp, stiffening its arms so he couldn't keep hold if he wanted to strike again. Just holding on proved to be a test of strength as it struggled like a caged animal, pulling and then pushing, and then bucking and twisting. It didn't stop moving for even a moment, jerking Shane every possible way to free itself.

The ghost's right arm broke free long enough for it to scratch a nail down Shane's neck. He caught it again quickly but could already feel blood flowing from the wound. The arm flailed and jerked and pulled free once more.

A cold hand caught Shane's face and squeezed. Fingernails dug into his cheek as the palm pressed over his lips. It pulled at him, sinking the nails in like fishhooks and Shane growled in pain as he let his body bend and collapse on top of the ghost. As its elbow reached its limits to extend and pull, Shane opened his mouth wide. Ghostly flesh brushed over his teeth, and he shook his head enough to get a grip and then bit down.

His teeth sunk into the freezing mass, sending a shockwave of pain through his nerves. His scream was muffled by a mouthful of the ghost's hand. Shane bit as hard as he could and pulled back. The ghost's hand spasmed and released him. His teeth tore the chunk of flesh loose between its thumb and forefinger.

Shane spat the ghostly flesh to one side just as a light in the distance cut through the darkness, momentarily blinding him. He had no time to worry about the source. Instead, he reached down and felt the cold, smooth flesh of the ghost, his fingers recognizing ridges and curves consistent with a face. It was hairless and bony, but he found the thing's left ear. His hand encircled it and pulled, lifting the ghost's head momentarily and then smashing it to the ground.

The ghost released Shane's other wrist to defend itself. Shane grabbed for the other ear and held it firmly, smashing the ghost's head into the ground again and again. He squeezed, applying pressure as the light in the dark came to a stop.

"Hey!" someone yelled, half in a panic. "Hey, hold on!"

There was a shuffling of footsteps and then something swung down right before Shane's eyes.

The form beneath him vanished, and he crumpled to the tunnel floor. There was nothing in his grip any longer. The mysterious light moved and focused on Shane, forcing him to cover his eyes.

"You mind?" he said, sitting up on his haunches. The light moved down.

"Sorry," a male voice said. The ghost had vanished. In its place, a piece of rebar stuck out of the tunnel floor.

Shane looked up. A shadowy figure held a flashlight, aiming it straight down.

"Oh, hold on," the shadow man said. He lifted the flashlight and pressed a button. The beam of light turned into a yellow emergency light and, with another button push, a lantern bar lit up, filling the space with soft, white light.

The man holding the light was young, maybe in his mid-twenties. He wore a blue hoodie and bulky, gray pants. One of his shoes was wrapped in duct tape.

"Jesus, you're bleeding," the man said. Shane lifted a hand to his face and pulled away bloody fingers. The ghost's claws had torn right through his cheek. He'd have a few fresh scars when the wounds healed.

"It's fine," Shane muttered. *Nothing too bad*, he thought.

"Fine? That thing kills people, man. Killed a lot of people."

Shane looked at the man. Under the hoodie, his blond hair was short and messy. His features were sharp, and his eyes were keen.

"You know what he is?"

The man shrugged uncomfortably.

"Well, I mean, it sounds stupid—"

"It's a ghost," Shane offered. The man was silent but nodded.

"Yeah," he said after a moment. "Most people don't believe in ghosts."

"Most people didn't have one almost claw their face off," Shane pointed out. He got to his feet and felt the wound on his neck. It wasn't deep, but it seemed to bleed a lot. He probably looked like a nightmare.

"You hit it with rebar?" Shane asked. The young man picked up the iron bar from the ground and hefted it like a baseball bat.

"Yeah. It's the only thing that works on it that I've seen. Doesn't kill it though. It always comes back."

"No. Iron doesn't kill them. They're already dead."

"Them?" the man asked.

"Ghosts," Shane clarified.

"All ghosts?"

"Yeah. How'd you know to use iron?"

"Luck, I guess," the man replied. "It came for me and a friend once, months ago. This rebar was the only thing handy, so I took a swing. Then it just vanished. Like a bubble, or something."

Shane grunted. The man was lucky the ghost hadn't come right back and gutted him on the spot. The iron would have sent it back to wherever it came from, popped back to the haunted item that bound it to the world. And it probably made the ghost mad. But not much else.

The young man looked at the rebar again, turning it in his hand.

"It's the iron that does it? This isn't like… from a church or something?"

"Just iron," Shane confirmed. "Sends it back to whatever it is bound to. Temporarily."

"Where did it come from?" the man asked. Shane shook his head.

"No idea."

Shane dusted himself off and looked around the tunnel now that he had more light. He turned in a circle while dusting himself off and retrieved the cigarette he planned to smoke earlier, lighting it with his Zippo.

"I'm Connor, by the way," the young man said, holding out a hand. Shane inhaled and looked the man in the eye before taking his hand.

"Shane," he replied. "Looking for a friend who might be down here. You know where people stay around Tremont?" he asked.

Connor smiled curiously.

"Yeah. I stay there. There's like a group of us. Who are you looking for?"

"A man named Martin. Canadian, about your age."

Connor nodded and looked around nervously.

"I know Martin. I can take you to him, but we should probably get going."

There was no telling how far away the ghost that attacked him had been sent, or if it was even going to return, but Shane agreed. He could deal with it later. He needed to find Martin first.

Connor kept the flashlight on in lantern mode and led the way back down the tunnel to the south. His pace was cautious, watching the shadows for any sign of the ghost along the way, while Shane walked next to him.

"How do you know Martin?" the man asked as they walked.

"Met him through work a while back," Shane answered.

"Isn't he an artist or something?"

Shane glanced at Connor. The other man was still watching shadows, scanning left to right as they went.

"Yeah," Shane said. "He did some work for me."

"How did you know he was here?"

"Got a call," Shane explained. "Has he been here long?"

"A little while, I guess," Connor replied. "Most people don't spend long down here. There's a handful of old-timers. The rest spend a few nights, maybe a few weeks, then move on."

"Where to?"

"Oh, wow," Connor said. "Who knows? Some move to another part of town. Some don't like being underground, so they just go up again, maybe a shelter or the park or something. Some just vanish."

Shane exhaled a puff of smoke.

"Vanish, as in…?"

"Vanish," Connor said again. "People who live down here don't leave trails. Most of them go by first name only, or a nickname. If a guy called Mouse who lives in a sewer disappears, he's hard to find again. Plus, no one goes looking."

"What about you? Why you wandering in a tunnel alone when you know there's a ghost down here who attacks people?"

"Was passing by and caught the flicker from your light," Connor explained. "I know it's bad news for people to be here. Figured maybe I could help."

He lifted his piece of rebar again as though weighing it and glanced at Shane.

"Lots of people go missing down here. But ever since I discovered I could hurt that thing, or at least make it go away… figured I should help if I can."

"Brave," Shane told him. "Stupid, too. If he wasn't distracted by me, he probably would have gone for you. Wouldn't have let you get in a swing with your rebar this time. Probably won't next time, either."

"I could have left you there," Connor pointed out. Shane would have destroyed it in another moment if Connor had left him there, but he didn't need to mention that.

"You could have," Shane agreed.

The blood on his face was drying and speaking pulled the wounds in his cheeks, making them sting. He'd need to find somewhere to clean up and maybe bandage them. He could taste blood in his mouth where the nails had pierced through.

"Are you here to take Martin home or something?" Connor asked, switching the subject.

"Not my home," Shane replied. "We're not that close. But he sounded like he needed help, so I came."

"Alright. I mean, you're not wrong. Martin's not doing so good. Not that anyone here has room to talk. This isn't the Langham Hotel; people are down here for a reason."

"The Langham, huh?" Shane said. "Never been there."

"Well, this is a downgrade," Connor said. "Lots of guys hear voices or are just drunk and high all the time. Some are violent. It's a bad place."

"Martin into any of that?"

"Drugs, you mean?" Connor asked before shaking his head. "Not that I have ever seen. He's on edge, though. I always figured he just had an illness that wasn't being treated."

"When Martin called, he told me about this ghost, too. Said it was killing lots of people. And he said it didn't want him here."

Connor nodded, still scanning the edges of the light.

"So, you're some kind of ghost hunter?" he asked. Shane exhaled smoke again.

"How much farther?" he asked.

"Not too far," Connor answered. "There's a passage off the next platform, and then it cuts through a broken wall to the storm sewer. Straight shot to the camp from there."

They traveled in silence for a moment before Connor started up again.

"Most people down here know about it. The ghost, I mean. Maybe not what it is, but that there's something. A boogeyman. A monster. Whatever they want to call it."

"So, it's no big secret, huh?"

"No. I mean, it's a couple dozen drunks, addicts, and lunatics having a meeting of minds. They know about it, but it's hard to say how many of them believe it's real or just can't think rationally anymore."

Shane chuckled at that.

"It is real," he said.

"Yeah. But I don't think most of the people here could handle knowing that for sure. I think everyone relies on everyone else being unreliable. Like Bigfoot sightings or UFOs. Everyone just pretends to believe the same thing when they never really saw anything."

Shane touched the wound on his face.

"Except for when someone goes missing because they've been torn to pieces and exploded like a blood balloon on a subway wall, huh?"

"I guess," Connor said.

It was a strange thing for the man to say, Shane thought. But maybe it was easier for people to cope with a harsh reality by secretly hoping there was a reason none of it was real.

Connor moved the flashlight to their left, holding it high as they approached a new platform and the tunnel widened into a large space.

"Here," he said. "This is the way to everyone else."

## Chapter 7
# The World Unseen

The smell in the sewer was not one Shane was happy to experience. He had hoped, being a storm sewer, he would only experience water. That was not the case. Several people had clearly been using the drains for dumping trash and going to the bathroom. Not to mention the occasional dead rat he saw floating bloated and rotten.

The place smelled of filth and decay. If there was any relief, it was in the presence of the rats, which at least showed that the ghost spent little time there.

"If everyone knows this place is dangerous, why are you still here?" Shane asked, trying to distract himself from the smell as they sloshed through the passageway.

"Like I said, everyone knows it but doesn't want to know it, if that makes sense. They're here because they want to be here. This place has shelter, privacy, and community. It's not the worst gig going in that regard."

"There's a ghost killing people," Shane said. It was the only fact that needed to be considered as far as he was concerned.

"People die every day. You can OD on the street, or get mugged, or beaten by a gang, or even cops. There aren't a lot of good options."

"Any option is better than being torn apart by a ghost."

"Only if you believe that's going to happen. Most people don't want to, even if they know it could. Some of these guys have been homeless for years. You can't convince them it's more dangerous here than up there," Connor explained, pointing at the ceiling.

Shane sighed. This was a world he didn't fully understand and didn't want to. He knew a lot of Marines ended up in similar situations. They had problems with drugs or alcohol or PTSD and no one to help them. For some people, maybe the street was the best option. Or the only option. He didn't want to judge Martin or anyone else for that. It wasn't about that. It was about what was being done to them.

"Any idea what this ghost wants? Why he does what he does?" he asked. Connor shook his head.

"Everyone has a theory. It's a black magic ritual. It eats people. It keeps them imprisoned. I can't see how anyone would know for sure."

"Never heard him speak?"

"I only saw it twice before. Never thought to ask it questions," Connor said.

He led them through another break in a wall onto a new set of tracks. The tunnel was brighter than the ones Shane had gone in, with faint light sources coming through from somewhere ahead.

He could hear voices in the distance, too indistinct to make out clearly but enough to know people were talking. As they approached a new platform, Shane could finally see people.

The platform was adorned with more of the rickety campsites that had been erected from random bits and pieces of junk. One looked like a small cabin made from old pallets while a few more were made from tarps or tents.

People huddled around small fires together, some in quiet pairs. In one central spot, a half-dozen men stood around a barrel fire, talking and laughing.

Shane couldn't get an accurate count on the number of people, but it was more than a dozen for sure.

Voices dropped from conversational tone to whispers as eyes fell on

Shane. Strangers were not a welcome sight, or a trusted one.

"Is he a cop?" someone asked loudly.

"He's not a cop," Connor replied.

"Looks like a narc," someone else offered. "Jesus, what happened to his face?"

"Cop, huh?" Shane said. That was a harsh criticism.

"They think everyone's a cop at first," Connor explained.

Near the end of the platform, a familiar face came into view. Huddled in front of a small tarp tent, Martin sat with his knees up. He was alone and sitting atop a rumpled sleeping bag. His dark hair was longer than Shane remembered, shaggy, and in need of a trim, and his face had thinned out beneath the scruff. He looked tired.

Martin's eyes locked on Shane, and he scrambled to his feet, coming to the edge of the platform as Shane climbed up.

"You came!" Martin exclaimed. He lunged at Shane and embraced him in a quick and unexpected hug. Shane stiffened, his arms straight at his side, and lifted them after several seconds when it seemed clear Martin would not release him soon.

Martin broke the embrace and took a step back. Their relationship had not even been a friendship, and it was certainly not one that involved hugs.

"Your face," Martin said, lifting a hand. Shane caught his wrist, gently but firmly, preventing him from touching the wounds caused by the ghost.

"It's fine."

Many of the others on the platform were eavesdropping on their conversation. From the corner of his eye, Shane had seen a couple slip down side passages already.

"I didn't think you'd come," Martin said. His eyes were wide, and he seemed unable to sustain eye contact for long. Instead, his focus darted about haphazardly.

"Sounded like you needed help," Shane replied. Connor stood with them though he said nothing, while Martin nodded.

"Yeah. Yeah. I mean, yes, I need help. It's not good. It's not good here," he said, rushing the words.

"Because of the ghost?"

It seemed like there was more going on with Martin than just the ghost, but a deadly spirit certainly improved nothing.

"The ghost. It's not good here," he said again. "Before. Um, when there was the other ghost, it was bad. The walk to your house, and then the basement, and he was in my head, you know? He was all that I could hear, and he never stopped. I never stopped. For days and days. I was just—"

"Martin," Shane interrupted, trying to regain the man's focus. Martin had been possessed by one of the strongest ghosts Shane had encountered, a being that was as angry as he was powerful. The impact that it had on Martin was worse than Shane realized.

"Yes," Martin said, focusing on Shane again. "It's hard to stay on track sometimes. Hard to say what I want. Connor here helped me. He helps me."

"That's good," Shane said, glancing at the other man.

"Yeah. Yes. He's good. He, um, he helps me. Oh! He said I should call you, and it was a good idea, I hope. It's dangerous here."

His eyes stared into Shane's, desperation on his face mixed with fear and an underlying confusion.

The Martin Shane had known, however briefly, was a bright and clearheaded young man. He was nothing like this. Lazarus had ruined that man.

"You need to leave, Martin. Go home. Go spend time with Big Bear or whoever else you have back in Canada."

"No. No, no," Martin said, shaking his head. "I can't go back there. I can't escape him there, you know? I know he's gone, but I remember. I can remember him there, and it feels like he's back. No. No, it's too…"

He shook his head to stress his point and Shane finally put a hand on his shoulder, drawing his focus back again.

"Alright. But you need to get out of here. Hell, go south. Stay somewhere warm. Winter has to suck in this place."

Martin looked at Connor and then back at Shane.

"But I can't leave with the ghost still here. It's going to keep killing people. I can't let it keep killing people. What if it takes one? What if it goes inside someone like Lazarus did to me and just stays there? In someone's head? I can't."

Shane sighed and nodded. The guilt was almost palpable. The fear that what happened to him might happen to someone else must have been overwhelming. None of it was Martin's responsibility, but Shane wasn't about to waste his breath trying to explain that. He didn't think Martin was in a place to handle too much rational thought, anyway.

"Who else here knows about this ghost? Really knows, not just the boogeyman thing?" Shane asked.

"A few people," Connor answered. "Lots of us have seen something. Or heard it. Or knew someone who went into the tunnels and never came back."

"Give me somewhere to start."

"You're gonna end up like Leon," a voice from behind said.

Shane turned and looked back to where the group of men around the barrel fire had stood. Two of them had left when Shane arrived, and a third left when Shane turned around.

An older man with white hair, a mustache stained yellow from years of smoking, and an olive-drab army jacket met Shane's gaze.

"Who's Leon?" Shane asked, leaving Connor and Martin for a moment to talk to the stranger.

"Was a pissant pickpocket," the man replied distastefully. "He was mapping all the tunnels down here. Getaway routes or some fool-ass thing. And look where that got him."

Shane raised an eyebrow and looked around.

"Where did it get him?"

"Dead, I reckon," the man answered. "Been missing for over a week now. Same as Patty, same as Billy Clips, and Droog and Cobb. They all went missing, no one seen hide nor hair since."

"What do you think happened to them?" Shane asked.

"You got a smoke?" the old man countered.

Shane pulled a pack of Lucky Strike from his pocket and retrieved one for the other man and one for himself. He lit them both with his lighter and waited while the old man took a slow drag, holding the smoke in his lungs for an unusually long time.

"I ain't had a Lucky Strike in years," he said at last.

"Army?" he asked, nodding to the man's coat.

"Second battalion, sixty-ninth armor regiment."

"Tanks?"

"Yes, sir," the man said. "You ever sit in the belly of an Abrams in the Gulf?"

"Never had the pleasure," Shane told him. "But I can imagine. Wasn't the most hospitable climate I've endured."

"You served?" the older man asked.

"I did."

"A jarhead," the man replied, nodding. "You look like a jarhead."

"I'll take that as a compliment," Shane nodded.

"Sergeant Lee Hamlin," the man said, offering half a salute. "Retired."

"Shane Ryan," he said. "Also retired."

"And now we're both in a hole in the ground that smells like piss talking about the boogeyman eating folks in the tunnels. Ain't that something?"

"It's definitely something," Shane agreed. "So, what do you know about this boogeyman?"

Hamlin took another long drag on his cigarette, his narrowed eyes hidden below bushy, white eyebrows. He exhaled out the side of his mouth.

"Directly? Not a hell of a lot. Just as well, too. I don't venture into the tunnels on account of I don't need to die screaming. Seen enough of that for one lifetime. But I know them other fellas that came looking. Thought you were one at first, if I'm being honest."

"Other fellas?"

"Yeah. Real class-A scumbag types. Kind of folks who use the people down here as bait."

"They were baiting the ghost with living people?" Shane asked. Hamlin nodded slightly.

"Oh yeah. Pulled all kinds of tricks. Offered money for people to be 'guides' in the tunnels. Came to help, they said. Like you. But they came in teams. Real slick when they come. Lots of trackers and tech and always at least one idiot in a nice, clean suit."

"Did they ever say who they were?"

Hamlin scoffed, grinning at Shane.

"Come on. These fellas weren't working for anyone legit; that was clear enough. But they flashed so much cash that most folks didn't care. They went into those tunnels with big wads of dough and never came back. Of course, most of them flashy fellas never came out either."

Shane took another puff off his cigarette, glancing around at the faces of the people who hadn't fled yet. Most pretended not to listen, but it was clear everyone still was.

"So, what makes you think I'm not one of those guys?"

"You came alone," Hamlin answered. "You got no gear. By the look of your face, you already got roughed up. And the first thing you did when you got here was to tell that boy to get out of here. Them other fellas never gave a damn about anyone down here. They didn't want to help us. They wanted to catch that ghost."

# Chapter 8
## Baiting Traps

Regardless of what had happened to Martin and the help he might have needed, he had been right about one thing. The ghost in the tunnels would keep killing if no one stopped it. In conversing with Hamlin, it was clear that the ghost had been down there for years.

Shane's initial plan was to help an old acquaintance and eliminate a threat. But Hamlin's tale added a twist to what he had been presented with. Though the old man didn't know who these strangers were, flashing money around while using humans as ghost bait, Shane had an idea.

The Cult of the Endless Night might have dried up in Boston after Randall West's death, but the description was them to a T. Rich, stupid, careless, and looking to catch a ghost. Shane couldn't imagine it was anyone else.

An individual ghost hunter would have been one thing, but organized groups were scarce. And something as obscure as a killer subway ghost in Boston would only be known to locals.

That people had come in search of Switchyard more than once meant he was well hidden. If he had been in the subway for decades, he might have died in the abandoned tunnels years before anyone living there now had arrived. His haunted item could have been lost to time, hidden, or even buried. The cult would have no way to find it without the ghost's help, and Switchyard did not sound like the helpful sort.

The allure was also right up the cult's alley. A killer, a boogeyman in dark tunnels. He didn't speak, and he didn't have any motive that anyone knew, he just killed. People like Randall West would have loved that. Another showpiece for the collection.

"When was the last time these well-funded hunters showed up looking for the ghost?" Shane asked Hamlin.

The two had shared most of his pack of cigarettes by that point, and the sergeant had loosened up, seeming to trust Shane enough to share stories without suspicion. Others were not so welcoming. At least half of the platform's population had made themselves scarce while Martin and Connor sat at Martin's tent, not far off.

"Can't say for sure," Hamlin said. "Five weeks? Not so long, anyway."

Shane nodded. That was after West had died for sure. After the Boston cell of the Endless Night was supposed to have been destroyed. If it was the cult, and it sounded like them, then James' information was not reliable.

"I will say they were a different lot that last time," Hamlin added after a second of thought.

"How so?"

"Not as slick. Less gear, but more cash. Asked a lot of the same types of questions the other fellas had asked a long time ago. Where does it haunt, what does it look like, all that basic stuff."

"Like they were new at it," Shane said.

"Like that," Hamlin confirmed.

The man's eyes had narrowed again and, though his mustache and beard were good at obscuring the lower half of his face, he had that tone in his voice like he was smiling. There was something about it all that he found amusing.

"What?" Shane asked. The other man shrugged.

"I just mind my business. I never wanted their cash, had a stink to it from day one if you catch my meaning. But that last crew, weren't but one fella who came out of that tunnel alive. He tore out of here covered in blood that wasn't his own. They went in a lot cockier than the original fellas."

"And this survivor? What happened to him?"

"Gone. Ran off. No one been back since."

"No cops?"

This time Hamlin did laugh, which led to a fit of coughing before he stopped.

"Jarheads. You got the look of a man who knows when he's asking a stupid question, but you asked it, anyway. Wonder why you might do that."

"Just curious," Shane replied. Hamlin shook his head.

"No, you're not. Can see it in your eyes. You got cards you ain't showing me. But if we were sitting and throwing chips on the table, I'd wager you know who these fellas are I'm talking about."

"I probably know them," Shane answered honestly. "Sounds like some people I had dealings with."

"Dealings, huh?" the old man said. "That's a polite word."

"More polite than they deserve."

"These fellas got a lot of people killed. I know most folks don't care about people like me. You got folks down here that need medication but have been off of it for years. Folks who can be violent and scary to those good people walking around above our heads, and I get it. Who wants to care about a drunk old bum or some junkie? But no one deserves to die like that, you get what I'm saying?"

"I do," Shane told him. He knew more than Hamlin would ever realize, of course. Better than anyone, probably. Shane had seen what a cruel and vengeful spirit could do firsthand. Repeatedly.

"So, I'm gonna need you to answer a question for me, Ryan," Hamlin said, lowering his voice.

"Shoot."

"Why did you come down here if you know what lives in the tunnels and you ain't one of these other fellas?"

Shane pulled another cigarette from his pack and handed it to the old man.

"Because I'm what those fellas are trying to be. I can get the job done."

"Oorah, Marine," Hamlin said with a grin. "Semper fi."

Hamlin offered another lazy salute and tucked the cigarette behind his ear as he wandered off to the only member of his original crew who hadn't ducked out when he started talking to Shane.

Shane returned to Martin and Connor, crouching down next to them by Martin's tent.

"What was Sarge on about?" Connor asked.

"Giving me the lay of the land," Shane answered. "What do you two know about the ghost-hunting crews that have tried to catch the ghost down here? Where they come from, who funds them, anything like that."

"He told you about them?" Connor looked behind them where Hamlin stood.

"Heard about them from ghosts in a different station. Said groups came down here a lot, looking for this ghost called Switchyard. They'd show up, they'd die, then it'd happen again. You guys ever see that?"

Connor glanced at Hamlin once more and then over to Martin.

"Yeah," Martin answered. "They were rich or something. Didn't have much to say to anyone down here, treated most of us like we were invisible once they got someone to take them into a tunnel."

"I saw them before, too," Connor added. "That time and a time before. I figured they were some people on one of those Haunted Boston tours looking for a gritty thrill."

"Haunted Boston?" Shane said. "I heard most of them died. I don't think Haunted Boston runs death tours."

Connor shrugged.

"I don't know. Why else were they here?"

"For the ghost," Shane answered. "To catch it."

"You can catch ghosts?"

Shane looked from Connor to Martin and back. Martin had cast his eyes down, looking uncomfortable at the conversation.

"Some people can. Takes about as much luck as it does skill sometimes, though. Sounds like these guys have neither."

"Guess they're not that bright," Connor added.

"Probably not. Did you see the ones who survived? Where they went, anything that could identify them?"

Martin shook his head, and Connor shrugged.

"No idea, man. But why does any of that matter?"

"Matters because someone has their eyes on this ghost. They've been using you and your friends as bait, and I doubt they've given up yet."

"Yeah," Connor said. "But if you can do what Martin says, you could find it first, right?"

Shane looked at the young man and nodded after a moment.

"If I can destroy him then yeah, it'll probably make these other guys give up on their hunt."

"But how do you find it? These guys have all kinds of expensive tracking gear, and they haven't been able to get it yet."

"These tunnels aren't endless. Besides, I imagine he's a little pissed at me by now after our last run-in. He'll probably be looking for me."

"Right," Connor said, nodding.

"Did the guys ever give any names?"

"None I remember," Connor answered. Shane pulled out his pack of cigarettes again and looked into it. After sharing with Hamlin, he only had two left.

"I need to get out of here for a few minutes. What's the easiest way in and out?"

"I can show you," Martin answered. "I want to get out for a walk, anyway."

"You want some company?" Connor asked, getting to his feet with the other two.

"No. No thanks. Maybe later," Martin answered.

"You sure?"

"We're good," Shane told him.

Martin led him down off the platform again and farther south toward a light source that came from another hole in the wall. It was only a few yards from the platform and led to a different section of storm sewer. This one smelled much better than the first Shane had entered, though it was still littered with trash. After a short, upward trek from the hole in the wall, it fed out into a large opening obscured by greenery.

Martin pushed a loose grate out of the way and then moved the vines and weeds. He then led them into a drainage ditch in a wooded area behind a ball diamond next to a residential neighborhood.

"Where the hell are we?" Shane asked.

"Few blocks south of Boston Common," Martin said. "It's usually safer to go in and out at night, but the ditch keeps this one out of sight. No one pays much attention to us coming and going. Not really."

"There a store nearby?"

"That way," Martin answered, pointing to their right. "Block or two."

Shane lit a cigarette and looked Martin in the eye.

"Gotta be honest, Martin, you don't look good or sound good."

"Thanks," the Canadian said with an awkward laugh. Shane shook his head.

"I'm serious. You need to get out of this place. If it's what Lazarus did—"

"I don't want to talk about it," Martin interrupted, anger in his voice.

"I bet. But if that's what's going on, it's going to be a rough go. You tell a doctor, they're going to think you're crazy. The only way you can get help is by pretending nothing happened that would make you need help. It's crap. It's not your fault, though. You need to get somewhere you can at least relax, wherever the hell that might be."

"I told you I can't leave," Martin said firmly.

"No, you said you're worried about the people here. I get that. But when that's not a problem anymore, worry about yourself."

"This ghost. It's… it's so angry."

Shane exhaled smoke and placed a hand on Martin's shoulder.

"For now. And it's going to be a lot angrier when I'm tearing it apart. Go take your walk and relax, alright?"

Martin nodded.

"Yeah. Yeah, I have to walk. I'll see you later, okay?"

He left without waiting for Shane's response, climbing out of the ditch, and crossing the tree-filled patch of land to the sidewalk. Shane did the same, heading in the other direction.

After he found a corner store and got himself a new pack of smokes, he took out his phone. Boston traffic was loud and crowded as he leaned against the outside wall of the store and lit a new cigarette, watching the world pass by.

The phone rang once before the line clicked.

"Shane?" James Moran answered.

"Yeah. Looks like the Endless Night is still alive and kicking in Boston," he said.

"You've made contact?" James replied, barely sounding surprised.

"Not quite. Got word of some flashy idiots with a lot of money hunting a ghost in the subway here. Been at it for years, it sounds like, but never with any success. Their last run was only a month or so back."

"I see," his friend said.

"I'm told the latest crew seemed a little green. Not up to speed on the job, but the same basic MO. They're using the homeless as bait, paying them to be guides to lure out the ghost."

"They don't know where to find it?"

"No. It's a fishing expedition. Sounds like they were maybe trying to triangulate a spot before the shakeup, and now a new team is starting from square one."

"In the subway system?"

"Abandoned subway system. And storm sewers," Shane confirmed.

"A job like that could take years if it worked at all. Do they even know what they're looking for?"

"Doesn't sound like it. They know the ghost, not the haunted item. Could be a pocket watch buried under a foot of cement for all I know."

"Why would they be so reckless? What's to gain?" James asked, sounding offended by the idea of such an uninformed hunt.

"They call the ghost 'Switchyard'. I had a run-in with him already. Would have destroyed him, but I got interrupted. This thing is mean. Fights like an animal and looks like he's just in it to kill."

"So, it's a perfect trophy for them," James said.

"Hempstead would have loved him," Shane added. Arthur Hempstead, the first cultist Shane had encountered, had a collection of rare and powerful spirits. He would have appreciated Switchyard's brutality.

"These people," James said with a sigh. "Let me see what I can learn. As I told you before, I heard that most of the upper echelon of the cult had fled town, but there are the lower ranks. And you said the last hunt was conducted by people who seemed uninformed. I'm wondering if some upstart is trying to leap into the hole left by the upper ranks and take control."

"Filling the power vacuum with a new generation of idiots," Shane suggested.

"Precisely. Just because someone was a low rank in the cult doesn't necessarily make them less dangerous," James pointed out. "These younger members might only have low rank because they were recruits. If anything, they could be more dangerous. Ambitious plus equipped with the cult's knowledge and resources, but none of their experience. That's a troubling mix."

"See what you can find out. I'll take care of the ghost, but I'd like to know if someone is trying to get the band back together in Boston and kick them in the ass now before they become a nuisance again."

"Will let you know. Do be careful, Shane. I'd hate to end up in a swamp with you again."

"The feeling's mutual," Shane added, hanging up the phone. As much as he had grown to detest the Endless Night, the prospect of getting to squash a potential uprising was enticing.

It would serve as a good lesson for the others in town and down south: Join the cult and face the consequences.

## Chapter 9
# The Hunt

By the time Shane finished his cigarette, his phone was ringing again. He answered, stripping down the butt as he did.

"That was faster than I expected," he said.

"There are fewer channels to go through to get information these days," James replied. "The information is not as detailed, either."

"What have you got?"

"A name. Enzo Colangelo. He's a collector in Boston. Not of any significant influence, but he dabbles, let's say. I think most of his interest lies in the more pedestrian albeit illegal trade of goods. At any rate, his name came up as it relates to the Endless Night. He's moving some items that once belonged to people like Randall West and Arthur Hempstead. That's the strongest link I have right now."

"Have an address?"

"I'll text it to you. I think this man is something just above a street-level thug so you may want to watch your back."

"Always," Shane said. He thanked James and checked the text he'd received. The address was not one Shane recognized, but it was in East Boston, beyond the Callahan Tunnel.

He wanted to let Martin know he was heading out and would be back later, but there was no way to contact the man. He just hoped he was smart enough to keep his distance from the tunnels until Shane was back to get things sorted.

Shane walked the several blocks back to Tremont, where he'd parked his car by the theater. He glanced into the park several times, briefly entertaining the idea of letting Jaker know he'd found who he was looking for, then decided against it. He'd give the ghost a heads-up when he was done in town.

Instead, he headed up through the tunnel toward the address James had provided. Shane knew people were trading in haunted items across the world. Most were not as cautious or knowledgeable as James Moran. But anyone who made a living doing it—with a heavy emphasis on living—had to have some kind of intelligence. There was no saying how long Enzo Colangelo had been in the business, however.

The drive to East Boston with midday traffic took Shane longer than he'd intended. He ended up near Orient Heights, not far from the harbor, in an ugly, industrial part of town. Colangelo's warehouse barely qualified for the name. It looked more like a rundown garage or small factory, with two loading bays and a graffiti-tagged front door that was plastered with more curse words per square inch than Shane would have thought possible.

The exterior of the building was mud brown and dirty cream-colored with trim the color of oxidized blood. There was one car, a mid-90s Toyota, in the cracked and uneven lot out front, parked against a small forest of weeds.

Shane parked next to the car and looked around. There was one security camera over the loading bays and the wire hung loose. The entire neighborhood had the depressing air of a place no one had cared for in at least a decade. Only a handful of cars traveled up and down the street, and there weren't even sidewalks for pedestrians.

The only sounds were from the William F. McClellan Highway two blocks to the west, which provided the constant hum of traffic and the odd horn honking.

Shane approached the front door of the warehouse and tried

the handle. It opened easily, swinging into a hallway that smelled like old coffee and microwaved dinners. The pile of gray carpeting was trampled flat and stained with salt and oil over years of use.

A hallway stretched out before him to another white door, but to the left was a small office with a glass one. Inside, a woman with tight red curls was smoking a cigarette over an ashtray that held at least a dozen butts and staring at a computer screen.

Bells chimed over the door as Shane pushed it open and stepped inside. The air conditioning had made the room a virtual ice box and smoke hung heavy in the air. The woman at the desk put her cigarette on the edge of the ashtray and smiled, showing candy-apple red lipstick.

"Can I help you?" she asked. He did not know if she was twenty years old or forty; she had a face that seemed to defy time. Her voice was friendly enough, however.

"Looking for Enzo Colangelo," he said. The woman nodded.

"Is Mr. Colangelo expecting you?" she asked, reaching for her phone.

"No. A friend suggested he might be able to help me find something."

"Fun!" the woman replied, pressing a button as she lifted the phone to her ear. "Mr. Colangelo, there's a gentleman here to see you."

She blinked once and nodded as she hung up the phone and then pointed a red-nailed finger at the door through which Shane had just entered.

"Down the hall to the white door. He's at the back of the warehouse, hun," she said.

"Thanks."

She resumed smoking as Shane left the room. For a place that dealt in haunted objects and potentially other illegal trafficking, it didn't seem very ominous. He wasn't sure smoking was legal in offices anymore, but other than that, Colangelo seemed to have an odd setup. The Endless Night had fallen on hard times if this was their new source for ghosts.

Shane pushed through the door at the end of the hall and was met with a new musty smell mixed with a heavier version of the coffee-and-microwave-dinner aroma of before.

The warehouse space was larger than he expected from the outside but by no means impressive. There were perhaps a dozen tables set up in the middle of the room on which hundreds of boxes were stacked. Several women stood on either side of each table, opening the boxes and sorting items that ranged from silverware to electronics to toys. Big plastic totes of similar-looking items were arranged around them.

The side and rear walls were lined with shelves, all stacked with still-sealed boxes that seemed to await their chance at being sorted.

At the rear of the warehouse, a short, stout man sat at a table drinking coffee and typing on a keyboard with one hand. He wore a cheap-looking blue suit strained around his blocky frame and a hideous Hawaiian-themed tie that didn't match at all.

At a glance, he looked like a wrestler from the golden age of the sport. One of those men built like a brick who would preen for the camera and then kick a man in the face with a boot laced up to his knees.

The man's mustache was thick and dark, but he had only the faintest wisp of hair on his head. He smiled as Shane approached, setting his coffee on the rickety table and getting to his feet.

"Hello, sir. How can I help you?" he asked, wiping his hands on his pant legs before holding one out to shake. Shane didn't take it.

"Enzo Colangelo?" he asked.

"You bet! Anything you need, I can get it for you. At cost or better! That's a guarantee. Mostly. What do you need, Mister…?"

"Shane Ryan," Shane said. Colangelo's eyes widened, and his expression became one of surprise, but not in the way Shane had expected. If anything, he looked delighted.

"Shane Ryan? Oh my God. You mean Shane Ryan *Shane Ryan*? THE Shane Ryan?" he asked. Shane was not sure how to answer and Colangelo leaned in, lowering his voice in a conspiratorial fashion.

"The Shane Ryan who messed up Randall West's entire operation?"

"You know West?"

"Never met him!" Colangelo said, raising his voice again and laughing. "But I knew of him. Not telling tales out of school to say I heard he was a real jackass. My business has gone through the roof since he went the way of the dodo."

"He was unpleasant," Shane agreed. Colangelo laughed again. It was a boisterous sound that turned his round face red with effort.

"Unpleasant, boy howdy. He was a real... well, you know. Is that why you're here? You in the market for some ghosts? I got ghosts. You want old ghosts? New ghosts? I just got a ghost from Barbados, swear to God, you can see his brain. It's disgusting. Oh, but he was a hoot to see at first, let me tell you."

Shane had not expected the man to have no qualms about sharing the nature of his business. Most people kept that part of their life under wraps. Colangelo was practically yelling.

"Do you work for the Endless Night?" he asked, cutting to the chase. Colangelo raised his hands, palms out.

"I'm an entrepreneur!" he replied. "I work for myself. But I have had business with that group. They throw money around like rice at a wedding, and who am I to say no to that?"

"Right," Shane said, looking around the warehouse again. "They ever come to you about a ghost in the subway near Tremont?"

"God, that again?" Colangelo replied with a chuckle. "They've been antsy to get their mitts on that Switchyard fella for a dog's age, haven't they? You'd think he was a Mickey Mantle rookie card."

"So, they've come to you about it?"

"I'll tell you what I told them. No one knows the ghost's name. He was spotted for the first time down there in 1897, so he was either on the construction crew or sneaked in during construction and then bought the farm. Fella's not a big talker though. He mostly likes to, you know—"

Colangelo made a face, sticking his tongue out of the corner of his mouth and running his thumb across his throat in a slicing motion. He couldn't get through it before laughing again.

"Have you tried to catch it for them?"

"Me? No sir, I'm no ghost hunter," Colangelo answered, slapping his stomach. "I went soft in my old age. But I got some supplies for them. Good price, too. You looking to go after him? I'll give you the same deal. Better even. You're Shane Ryan!"

Shane shook his head.

"Let's go back to them needing supplies. How often are these guys you're talking about trying to catch him?"

"Last run was a few weeks back. I can check the files if you need a specific date."

"No," he said. "What did they need from you?"

"Usual stuff people want for ghost hunting. Spectrometers, EVP recorders, EMF meters, holy water-infused body armor, silver nets, the whole bit."

Shane stared at the man waiting for another laugh that didn't come.

"Holy water-infused body armor?" he asked. Colangelo shrugged.

"I get it from Italy. Standard-issue Kevlar stuff that law enforcement gets, plus holy water from a church in Rome. Costs about twelve grand per set. You want some?"

"They pay you for that?"

Colangelo's smile turned sly.

"If I can sell a prop from Ghostbusters and turn a profit, I'm going to do it."

"How many of those guys died as a result?" Shane asked.

"Do you care?" the other man answered. Shane did not. But Colangelo's nice-guy routine had quickly taken a dark turn. Now he was showing off some of the danger that seemed to be part of what James had warned about.

"Do you know how close they got to Switchyard?"

"Look, friend, I like you. You made me a wealthy man in these past couple of months. With West gone and most of his yahoo friends with him, the riffraff has been desperate to get to the head of the pack, and they've all come to the only game in town—yours truly. But I can't go ratting out my clients to anyone who comes knocking."

Shane was about to level an idle threat, but Colangelo continued.

"That said, maybe we can work out a deal. You keep me in the loop about your work in town, I keep you in the loop about mine?"

"I could agree to that," Shane said. There was no reason to be fully honest with him, of course. But he had the distinct feeling Colangelo was not an honest man, either.

"So, you're in town looking for Switchyard?"

"He came up on my radar," Shane confirmed.

"Think you can catch him?"

"I don't catch ghosts," he clarified. Colangelo grunted.

"Heard that. You got some trick to kill 'em off once and for all."

"No tricks. And they're already dead. I just make sure they don't bother people again."

"A valuable skill," the other man said.

"So these Endless Night guys?"

"I had some buyers. Knew it was them, though they didn't announce it. Not anyone in charge, just some helper monkeys, I'd wager. But they paid for the gear in cash on the spot."

"How'd you know who it was for if they didn't identify themselves?" Shane wanted to know.

"There's a new fish in the pond. Making it known he's running the show now. Don't have a name for you, before you ask. But there are stirrings I'm hearing about."

Shane mulled over the man's words. If they were running their operation through a guy like Colangelo, then it spoke to the level of disorganization left in Randall West's wake. Whoever had stepped up was at the amateur level, which made them potentially even more dangerous. It was someone without even the basic level of skill and savvy West had.

Someone trying to traffic in ghosts using unreliable and ineffective gear bought from a third-rate supplier was going to keep getting people killed. Not just their men and the homeless they victimized, but potentially many more. Passengers on the nearby subways were at risk, even random people on the street.

All it would take was someone pushing Switchyard too far. The ghost was already violent and dangerous. The only upside was that he liked to stay hidden underground. If the Endless Night kept encroaching, maybe that would change. Maybe he'd move to tunnels that were in use.

From there, the ghost needed only set up shop on a train that was in motion. Based on what Shane had experienced, Switchyard could turn a subway car into a meat grinder. No one would get out alive.

"Do you know where they're operating from? An address you send stuff to or anything like that?" Shane asked. Colangelo shook his head.

"They come to me. No big paper trails in this line of work, you understand."

"Yeah," Shane said. He had a sense the man was probably holding back some things, but he didn't expect any less. There was a slimy quality to him that made Shane think he'd sell his mother out for the right price.

"You going to tell them I was here looking into this?" Shane asked.

The big man laughed, his face going red again.

"Depends on the equation, doesn't it?"

"Equation?"

"How much they are willing to pay me for that information over how likely they'll get violent upon hearing I talked about them to someone else."

"Right," Shane said while Colangelo laughed. "Thanks for your time."

Colangelo offered Shane several discounts on ghost-hunting gear as he walked out before inviting him to come back anytime. He didn't bother to reply.

## Chapter 10

# Back Down

Shane exhaled one final lungful of smoke, leaning against his car at the side of the road. Half a block away, a man walked a French bulldog while talking on his cell phone. Cars passed, and the world kept on turning. No one paid attention to Shane, to the ball diamond in the park, or to the tree-enshrouded ditch that led to a storm drain.

No one had come in or out of the drain in the few minutes Shane had stood there, not that he expected to see anyone. He didn't know if Martin had returned. It didn't matter; he could talk to him later.

Shane had stopped to pick up a flashlight before coming back. After talking to Colangelo, it seemed clear that the only path forward was to destroy Switchyard. The Endless Night had been after the ghost for years, and even in the wake of their apparent destruction, nothing had changed. Anyone affiliated with the cult probably knew of the ghost. They would always keep coming.

Switchyard was some kind of white whale, a trophy they refused to leave alone. His enigmatic nature would have appealed to their foolish, greedy minds. Silent, deadly, rare, and seemingly impossible to catch. It was the ultimate status symbol for them. And even as they used innocent victims as bait, and sacrificed their own men, the desire probably grew.

Eradicating the Endless Night was harder than getting rid of cockroaches, but getting rid of the things they wanted was in Shane's wheelhouse. If he couldn't convince them all to leave for rational reasons, he could at least starve them out.

He finished the cigarette and locked his car. No one was around to notice as he ventured across the grass and into the tree-lined gully. He slipped into the storm sewer and sealed the weed-covered grate the same as Martin had left it before heading back below ground.

The place Martin and the others had chosen was well hidden, Shane realized, as he descended. A stranger stumbling upon the place had to head down a slippery decline for several yards before it leveled out. From there, the storm sewer continued north for a good distance before the break in the tunnel. A person could have continued forward or traveled through the break in the wall as Shane did, retracing his steps from earlier. But the break led to a darker tunnel, and those not familiar would likely be disinclined to want to risk leaving what seemed like the "real" path.

In the second tunnel, the darker path only went a short distance before the next break, which led to the old subway lines. It would be difficult to find in the dark. In the light, it was just as uninviting as the first broken path, a pile of rubble around a hole that could have been manmade or could have resulted from a collapse.

There were no sounds below that were unexpected or out of place. No voices traveled so far, only the soft and muffled noises of a city above and beyond, through layers of brick and earth. The hum and rumble of cars and trains and pipes.

Shane returned to the old platform where Martin and the others had made camp. Martin's tent was empty, and a few of those who had left when Shane arrived had returned.

Sergeant Hamlin was still huddled around the fire with a pair of his friends. He offered Shane a nod when the two made eye contact, but no one spoke to him, nor did he expect them to.

Rather than climbing up to the platform, Shane continued down the tracks. He wasn't concerned with the living. He wanted to find Switchyard.

There was little chance the ghost might listen to reason. He was a killer, and he seemed to enjoy what he did. He'd been at it for more than a century down there in the dark. That sort of thing was more than just a hobby; it was nature. It was who and what Switchyard was. There was no way to reason with that. He needed to be destroyed.

*The sooner the better*, Shane thought. To save Martin and his friends, and to force the Endless Night further away from their goals. He'd stomp this new group out before they could get a foothold and try to bring back what was lost.

Some of the homeless murmured among themselves as Shane passed, heading for the dark tunnels. Just as Connor had said, they all knew what waited back there. Even if they felt safe on their platform, they knew death was breathing down their necks in that place. And that Shane was going to meet it head-on.

He made his way back to the rancid-smelling sewer, careful to avoid any deep patches of water or piles of sludge. The flashlight made things worse. It was better not to see what he was stepping through, but he kept it on, anyway.

Shane reached the break in the wall and left the sewer for the dark tunnel where he'd first encountered Connor and the ghost. It was as cold as he remembered and deathly silent as he ducked through the broken brick wall.

He swept the beam of white light from left to right across the tunnel. The subway continued to Shane's left, deeper underground where he had not been before. The light showed little beyond scattered piles of rubble, dirt, and old cobwebs. Nothing moved.

He directed the flashlight down the tunnel where Switchyard had first attacked him. It was still and silent as well, no signs of movement or any indication that someone else had been there since.

Switchyard was the kind of ghost that liked to stalk, from what Shane had heard and seen. He didn't need to hide, but he still chose to. He liked to surprise his victims, prey on them, and instill fear alongside pain. It was not a unique trait among ghosts, but it wasn't exactly the norm.

Hunting a ghost that preferred to be the hunter was never easy. This one also knew the territory much better than Shane. Better than anyone. He had been there more than any natural lifetime. He would know all the secrets, all the hiding places and passageways. Shane was a fly wandering into a spider's web in the hopes the spider would be too arrogant to think it was in danger.

Shane chose the left path, deeper into the abandoned tunnel system. He needed to get some idea of the lay of the land, even if it was just basic. The goal was to destroy Switchyard, and if he could learn more about his habits and where he spent his time, that would only help. The Endless Night had been trying to do the same for years and still came up with nothing.

Just because the Endless Night had not found Switchyard didn't mean they hadn't learned anything. They knew enough about ghosts to understand their limitations. That told Shane that they had picked the location near Martin and his people for a reason.

If men under West and now under this new leader kept coming to that part of the tunnels, then they had triangulated the ghost's location enough to determine it was the prime spot to find him. West might have been ignorant of a lot of things, but the Endless Night was good at catching ghosts. The massive collections Shane had seen proved that.

They were not adept at handling large groups safely, but they knew enough to have tracked down some extremely unusual spirits in the past. They had resources, including things like Thomas Coulson, to draw from. If they kept going to Tremont, it was for a reason.

Shane kept a brisk pace as he delved deeper into the abandoned subway. He was not rushing, but he suspected there was no reason to pore over every inch of the tunnel. There was little chance any obvious thing was sitting out in the open that no one else had seen before.

He wasn't looking for Switchyard's lair or haunted item or anything of that nature. Those things were hidden and had eluded discovery for too long. They were immaterial, anyway. If Switchyard had some hidden room or secret hole in the ground, Shane couldn't have cared less. He wanted to lure the ghost out, that was all. He could destroy him anywhere.

The closer he was to whatever qualified as the ghost's stomping grounds, however, the better. So, staying in the vicinity seemed best. Even if he had a mile radius to travel, the Endless Night had determined the tunnels near Tremont were the best, and the stories seemed to support that. Shane was in the middle of Switchyard's kill zone. Just where he wanted to be.

Distant trains rattled and hummed in the walls. Dust shook loose in puffs and clouds. Sometimes, stones tumbled from walls, a threat of future collapses and potential disaster.

Shane stopped to pull out a cigarette, holding the flashlight under his arm as he did so. Somewhere, the squeal of train brakes rang out. He held the cigarette between his lips as he raised the lighter. The flash of flame filled his field of vision and everything beyond was swallowed by darkness as his pupils narrowed.

For just a moment, less than a heartbeat between his finger pushing down on the spark wheel and the flame coming to life, there was something there. A pale face, low to the ground in a crouch, watching him from the far side of the tunnel.

Shane pulled the flashlight from under his arm, swiping the beam through the dark like he was slashing out with a sword. The light bathed the wall where he had seen the ghost, like a spotlight on the stained brick, but nothing was there.

He inhaled, holding the smoke for a moment, and moved the light in a slow, steady arc. There was no sign of movement, no sign of the wan and waxy face he had thought he had seen just beyond the flame.

The air was still and chilled, as it had been since he arrived. He held his body still and calm, feeling the cold on his flesh. There were no gusts, no sense of movement, or a temperature drop.

Shane turned, sweeping the area behind himself and all around. Nothing. To most people, it would have been a trick of the eye, he was sure. They would have dismissed it as nerves, maybe nothing more than shadows playing in the light. But he knew better. Switchyard was watching him from somewhere near.

"Not coming out to play again?" Shane asked.

Smoke billowed from his mouth as he spoke. He was familiar enough with ghost scare tactics to have guesses of what would come next. A flash of movement at the edge of the shadows, perhaps. A sound. A gust of air. Anything to heighten tension and fear. Anything to make Shane panic. It wouldn't work, but the ghost didn't know that.

Shane kept walking. His body was tense, his muscles at the ready. Deeper into the tunnel and into the darkness he went. The air grew colder, and the distant trains became quieter until the sound of his pulse in his ears overwhelmed them.

A brick fell, the sound of rolling rock filling the nearly silent space with all the power and presence of an avalanche, drawing Shane's attention to the path behind him once more. The chunk of a pale-yellow brick rolled to a stop several paces from him. He caught it in the beam of light and looked beyond.

Switchyard was crouched low, his body mostly obscured in a small alcove in the brickwork. One white-and-purple-lined hand was pressed flat to the brick wall, as though the ghost were holding itself steady. Only half of his face was in view, a single white eye staring at Shane from within the gaunt, waxlike flesh.

His skin seemed translucent along the surface, a spider's web of purple veins like gossamer threads visible beneath. Some were thick as worms, like the one rising up the ghost's temple; others were barely visible.

His lips had been torn from his face, leaving only raw meat behind, not quite scabbed over, left swollen and pulpy. The inside of his mouth looked worse, the gums and teeth mulched like he had eaten a mouthful of razor blades. The ghost's nostrils flared like he was sniffing the air, a beast smelling the scent of prey.

The curled gray and black nails dug into the wall, and Shane stepped toward him. The ghost scuttled back, and Shane stopped. Switchyard stopped as well, choosing a small mound of fallen brickwork to shelter himself from view.

Shane moved to take another step, and the ghost backed off again.

"Well, then," Shane remarked, staying where he was. "Looks like you can teach an old dog new tricks after all."

He knew Switchyard didn't speak, and after seeing his mouth, Shane wasn't surprised. But his reactions didn't require an explanation. The ghost was keeping his distance. Despite being dead, he was still cautious. His choice of victims painted him as an opportunist. He didn't want to fight; he wanted to kill. He wanted it to be easy. And Shane was not an easy target.

Switchyard had learned that Shane could fight back, and now would not allow him to get close. There was some advantage in that, Shane was sure. The ghost was wary. Maybe not afraid, but he didn't want to risk being hurt. But there were downsides as well. If he didn't want a confrontation with Shane, then he would either avoid him like he was doing now or wait for what he thought was an opportune moment. Some time when Shane was distracted or unable to fight back.

There was something Shane didn't understand. The ghost didn't have to let him know he was wary. He didn't have to show up at all.

It made Shane wonder what the hell Switchyard was up to.

As if reading the expression on Shane's face, the ghost lifted his head above the pile of rubble and smiled. His body was smooth and hairless, like some lizard that had never seen the light of day. The pulpy, bloody mouth spread wide.

He raised a fist, white like the belly of a fish, and slammed it against the brick wall at his side. Dust fell in a sheet from the ceiling and bricks tumbled. The sound was like a hammer blow.

Switchyard's hand pounded against the wall faster and faster. Bricks fell along a long, cracked seam Shane had not noticed in the poor light. They fell loose from the wall from one side of the tunnel to the other, freeing them all.

Dirt and rubble followed as the ceiling collapsed. Dust plumes filled the light, turning the tunnel into nothing but a misty brown-and-black cloud.

Shane backed off, escaping the expanding heap of rubble and rain of stone. What started as a single line of brick became panels of it, yards of ceiling falling as the soil and stone under which the tunnel had been dug came crashing down. The sound was thunderous.

He turned and ran, the dirt flowing like a wave of water behind him until it finally seemed to plug itself, filling the tunnel to the ceiling. Shane was unsure how far he had run or how much rubble blocked his path as the final bits tumbled down the wall of dirt that spanned the entire width of the tunnel. He knew there would be no way to dig through.

*Thirty feet?* he thought. Maybe. He had acted more on instinct than anything. It had been too fast. Switchyard had tricked him, had lured him to the perfect spot. Now, he was trapped in a tunnel he'd never entered before.

And the only person who knew his location was the ghost who wanted him dead.

## Chapter 11
## The Lost Places

Shane's cell phone had no reception; not that he'd expected it to work. He would be on his own, as the ghost had planned. Shane sighed and retrieved another cigarette from his pack.

He used the flashlight to sweep the tunnel ahead. While there was a chance Switchyard would try to attack him, he didn't think it was likely. Trapping him in the tunnel was the plan, left to get lost or simply die with no way out. But that depended on what still lay ahead, Shane knew. And whether he could discover another way out.

The best-laid trap would have been to keep Shane in an inescapable tunnel where he'd die of dehydration in a few days. But Switchyard's trap had been impromptu. It was luck that Shane showed up, and that meant there was still hope. The tunnel ahead could have had branches and pathways, more broken walls, even an exit to the surface. He just had to find those things.

His steps echoed differently in the tunnel now that he was cut off. The air smelled different, mustier with all the dirt and silt that had fallen. He kept his pace brisk, now focused not on discovering the ghost but on anything that might help him find a way out.

Shane was unsure what Switchyard was thinking of. There was something about the ghost that was less than human. Being dead contributed to that, but this was a deeper affectation. Even the way the ghost had retreated from him when he stepped toward him. It reminded

Shane of wild animals. Not an apex predator, the sort of animal that stood up to a challenge. More like a carrion eater or scavenger. Something like a coyote, perhaps.

Switchyard wanted easy kills. He wanted to hide and have prey come to him in the easiest way possible. It didn't matter that he was a ghost and most people would never see him and certainly never fight back as Shane had. Something in his mind made him want to reduce the confrontational aspect of his hunts.

It was possible that the Endless Night hunting him had made him more cautious, but Shane didn't think that was it. This was an old ghost. He'd developed this behavior long in the past and had refined it.

In all likelihood, Shane would never understand why Switchyard was the way he was. The ghost couldn't or wouldn't talk. That was part of it, too. Part of that loss of humanity. Dying was just the starting point for many ghosts, where they slipped out of who and what they used to be. From there, many of them sank deeper with time.

If Switchyard had died in the tunnels when they were first being built, then he would have been trapped in the darkness for more than a century. Alone and mad and full of violence and rage. Small wonder that there was little left of him that seemed human. No one even knew his name. He was Switchyard, a convenient nickname for a thing that hunted people in a place abandoned even by the trains he once knew.

Shane would have to adjust his thought process. Switchyard was cunning, but he didn't think like other ghosts. This would be like hunting both man and animal in one. It would be a challenge. And one that could get him killed if he wasn't up to it.

Ahead, the darkness gave way to a new obstacle. A wall. Shane had reached the end of the abandoned tunnel. There was an old station here, another platform that looked older than any he'd seen so far.

The signs on the walls were rusted beyond recognition, and the clutter on the platforms had rotted away. No one had set up a shantytown here. No one had been here at all from what Shane could see. The dust had grown, layer upon layer, until it formed a mat of detritus.

Shane could see a set of stairs leading up to his left, but the rusted handrails and grimy concrete steps ended in a sealed and rusted door that bore the telltale signs of welds along the seams. It had been permanently sealed from the other side.

The right side of the platform looked much the same. Stone pillars were caked in years of grime and mold. There were no stairs teasing the idea of salvation. There was only a door.

He climbed up onto the platform, scanning the area with the flashlight. No trash piles, no sign that the platform had ever seen human life at all. A single door was near the end of the line, close to the welded exit, and it was narrow. Not the welded double doors of the exit, but a door to a room perhaps, or a passageway.

Flakes of green paint still held to the rusty iron. The keyhole was blocked with something, maybe just years of accumulated rust, and the knob refused to turn when Shane tried it.

He banged against it, and the sound was hollow. There was open space on the other side. It wasn't much to go on, but it was all he had.

Shane took a step back and lifted his foot, kicking the door with the bottom of his boot right next to the knob. The door rattled, rust and paint flaking off in a rain. He kicked again, and the sound boomed through the darkness.

Three more solid kicks and he stopped for a breather, checking the door. It rattled more easily, shaking in the frame as he pulled on the knob. It would give way if he kept it up, it was just not a fast process.

Shane kicked again and again. With a grunt of frustration, he changed his technique and took a run at it, leading with his shoulder. Metal groaned and something snapped. The door swung open, nearly causing him to take a header to the other side as it slammed against the interior wall.

He stumbled, catching his balance, and stood at the entrance to a dark, musty hallway. It smelled like mold and was strangely warm and humid compared to every other place Shane had come across up to that point.

The light showed a hallway lined with doors. It looked its age but reminded Shane of an old office building. The doors inside were wood, not metal, and the ones he could see had rotted with age.

The brass door handles were tarnished nearly black, and the walls had extensive growth. Piles of dead bio-matter lined the floor, generations of old fungus if he had to guess. Some doors still bore the latest spores, feeding off whatever nutrients were left in the damp, old wood.

Shane made his way down the hall. He kicked at the first door on his left, his foot easily putting a hole right through the wood and exposing a small office on the other side. It was empty of all but shelves and fixtures, including what looked like a small chandelier and bronze switch covers, all tainted by age.

The next room had to have been a supply closet based on the size and layout, and the room after that was another office. At the end of the hall before it branched right, the temperature had increased, and the humidity had become cloying. The door fell off its hinges when Shane pushed at it, revealing a bathroom on the other side.

Warm, dank air hit him in the face, the smell foul enough to make him step back. The interior of the room was like a living thing under the beam of his flashlight. There was a trio of stalls and sinks, and it had probably been covered in white tile at one point. Now, it was buried in fungus and mold. The water supply had never been cut off, and a pipe had burst at some time, leaking warm water.

Shane could hear the trickle of water down a drain, barely more than a few drips that never stopped. However long it had been leaking, it had given rise to a new ecosystem of murky things that looked like lumps of black and brown slime across every inch of the place.

He stood still, the beam of light coming to rest on something slumped in the farthest corner. He could make out the features even in the overgrowth of fungus. The pits where eyes and a nose had once been. The hands and the feet, stained with years but plucked clean of all traces of flesh.

The skeleton had become part of the room, part of the growth that consumed the place. Thick, bulbous ridges grew across the skull and along the arms. It almost looked like the fungus was giving birth to it when the truth was, it was still consuming it. In another few years, the whole thing would likely be covered completely.

There was no telling how long the body had been there. Not since the place was closed; someone would have noticed. Had it been Switchyard who killed the man? If it even was a man? Had the person fought to escape the ghost and cracked a small pipe in the melee, only to set up this putrefied corpse-recycling operation as the fungus ate the body and the rest of the room? Anything was possible.

Only one stall wall remained solid, to the left of the corpse, and as Shane watched, a series of thin, black tendrils trailing a stiff, smoky cloud slowly wrapped around the edge.

He held his ground, waiting for what was to come. The ghost moved with an impossible slowness, like a cat rising from a slumber. The haze-enshrouded hand held firm and a head came into view as though trying to spy around the edge at whoever had disturbed the door.

Though the beam of light did not waver in his grip, Shane felt the muscles of his arm tense. In his life, he had seen the horrors of death a thousand times over. He'd seen ghosts of people drowned in murk or burned beyond recognition. He'd seen spirits whose bodies had been ground into little more than meat, no longer recognizable as something that had ever been living or human. But he had never seen such a thing as he saw in the subway bathroom.

The spirit's body was beset with a slow-moving haze of particles. Only after seeing the whole being did he realize they were spores. Fungal spores, floating like a thick mist all around the body. Had it not been shaped like a man, he might not have guessed that was what it had once been.

A spectral fungus had consumed the spirit from head to toe. Huge bulges of ridged, black-and-cream-colored growths bloomed from the sides of the head and neck, some as large as a second head.

There were clusters of different growth. Some were small and the color of blood, growing in little caps across where the jaw should have been. Some were pale like maggots, and grew long and thin, almost like hair, across the shoulders and torso. Others were squat and wide, in shades of brown and orange.

It was a man in shape alone. There were no features to speak of. The head had no face. No mouth or nose or eyes. All was consumed and hidden beneath the layers of life that grew from death.

The ghost created a sound, maybe an attempt at speech. It was wet and rumbling. It made no move toward Shane now that it was out and potentially able to see him. It stood over its skeletal remains while he watched it.

"Just looking for a way out," Shane told the ghost. The bubbling hum came from its body once again. Slowly, purposefully, it raised its left hand and pointed to the right. Shane looked down the hall in the same direction. Doors, he could see, and another branch to the left at the end.

He turned back to the fungal ghost, shining the light toward it.

"I can... do you need help?" he asked.

It made a sound again, softer and lower, and then crept back behind the wall, out of sight once more. Shane said nothing, watching it go only a moment longer.

He stepped away from the room, taking the hallway to his right. He didn't bother with the next several doors as each seemed to be nothing more than offices or storage spaces. It must have been some sort of subway administration office once upon a time.

The hallway branched left and the door at the end of the hall was not wood this time. It was another green-painted metal door, like the one that had led him into the place, and he picked up the pace toward it.

This door was in better condition than the previous one, but only just. The humidity had taken its toll over the years and the rust, especially in the locking mechanism, had grown into a thick, rough-looking blossom of disfigured metal.

Taking up a solid stance, Shane kicked at the door. The metal groaned, but the door held firm. He was working against the lock and the hinges now. The work would be harder and potentially longer.

Before he could lift his foot to plant another kick, something hit the door from the opposite side. The bang was loud and solid, something hard slamming with a lot of force. The door shook and rust flaked away. Shane took a step back, flashlight in one hand, the other balled into a fist.

"Shane?" a muffled voice called out. He exhaled, cocking his head to one side. The voice was familiar.

"Shane, is that you?" Connor asked. His rescuer had found him in the tunnels yet again.

## Chapter 12
# Unmasked

Metal whined as it bent and split. The head of an ax sheared through the rusty surface and the lock broke apart. The door pushed open just inches then stalled, then moved a few more inches, and then stalled again, the built-up rust on the hinges and in the frame causing it to scrape and freeze up.

"Thank God," Connor said, his face coming into view in the gap he'd opened. "Help me with this."

He used his shoulder to push on the door again while Shane took the edge and pulled, helping him open it wide enough to pass through.

"Can't believe I found you," the man said. He held a red fire ax in one hand and his lantern flashlight hung from a strap over his other shoulder. He was alone.

"Yeah," Shane said, looking at the empty platform beyond him. "Hell of a thing."

"I was at camp and Sarge said you'd gone to the tunnels. I heard the cave-in and came to see what happened. I was afraid you'd been crushed or something, but I circled back to see if you got through."

He was breathing heavily and leaning on the door, a wide smile on his face. Shane glanced at the platform again. It was like the one he'd just left behind, crusted in old dust with no sign anyone had been there in years. Except for several sets of footprints.

Connor's were new, but there were other prints. People had been there some time ago. A month? Two months? It was hard to guess, but it was not years, Shane was certain.

"So you heard a cave-in and just grabbed an ax and ran around these tunnels to an abandoned station and found me here," Shane said. Connor's breathing slowed and the smile on his face remained frozen.

"Yeah, I guess so," he said.

Shane nodded, looking back the way he'd come before heading out onto the new platform with the other man. He shone the beam of his light down the tunnel, the way Connor's footprints showed he'd come.

"So, where's this go?"

"Connects back near where I first met you," he said.

"Convenient for us then," Shane said.

He could feel the tension he'd caused, and Connor had picked up on it. He looked at the ax in the other man's hand.

"No rebar this time?" he continued. Connor shrugged, hefting the ax to his shoulder.

"Wasn't thinking about it."

"You thought of bringing an ax. For a cave-in of rocks."

"No," Connor said. "Just in case you were trapped. I mean, it's all I had handy."

"Sure," Shane said.

He looked down at the platform again, at the older footprints that were partially dusted. He followed a set with the beam of his flashlight, across the platform to the far corner near a wall where whoever had made them had shuffled about.

Shane's flashlight rose, the beam climbing the wall until it stopped on a small, black box fixed in the corner. The light reflected off a tiny lens.

"Would you look at that," he whispered. Connor looked up.

"Camera?" he asked. Shane grinned, shining his light on the other man's face.

"Come off it, already," he said. Connor's smile wavered.

"I don't know what you mean."

"Sure you do," Shane told him. "How about you fill me in on the plan?"

Shane was willing to buy Connor's first appearance during his fight with Switchyard being a coincidence. And his story about discovering that iron could send the ghost away could have been plausible, too. But too many things built from there made his act fall apart.

Martin had said Connor was the one who encouraged him to call Shane. Connor had seemed eager at the idea of Shane being able to catch Switchyard. And now, showing up with an ax in the right place at the right time in what would otherwise be a hopeless maze to anyone else? None of it made sense. Unless Connor wasn't who he said he was.

"I don't—" Connor began. Shane's fist silenced the rest of the lie as it crunched into the man's nose.

He collapsed. Shane bent over, picking up the ax and resting it over his shoulder as Connor held his face, blood pouring in a steady trickle down his cheeks before he sat up.

"You broke my nose!" he yelled into the hand he clenched over it.

"That was the plan," Shane confirmed. "I'll break a finger next."

Connor scowled at him from behind the hand holding his nose.

"You think you can—"

The ax hit the ground between the man's legs. Metal on concrete rang through the station and echoed down the abandoned tunnel like a bell.

"I'm not interested in wasting time," Shane pointed out.

"Fine," Connor said. "What do you want to hear? I want Switchyard. The resources I've put into this? He's mine; I earned him."

"That a fact?" Shane asked. The man lowered his hand tentatively and spat blood into the dust.

"That's a fact. I lost a lot of men hunting this thing."

"More than Randall West?"

"Randall West was a rich deviant who lived like a selfish little king in his mansion. He knew nothing about getting his hands dirty. I'm willing to do the work. I always have been, but I never had the chance until now."

"Until everyone else left town," Shane clarified. Connor nodded.

"Yeah. Until you scared everyone off. We should work together, man! I'm not trying to run the world here. I just want to make some money. Do you know what the standing offer is for Switchyard? I can get thirty million for him tomorrow. More if I can provide proof of his age and the victims he's killed."

"Fascinating," Shane said.

"It is," Connor countered. "We could be rich. The money you leave on the table every time you go after a ghost should make you cry, man. In a year, with my help, you could make eight figures. Nine, even."

"Bet all the guys who died helping you would be happy to hear that," Shane said. Connor wiped blood off the back of his hand.

"Risk versus reward. No one is here by accident. They all get it. Football players risk concussions. Drivers risk crashes. Even astronauts risk catastrophe every time they take a mission. This isn't any different."

"No one playing football is going to run off the field and murder a random fan in a subway tunnel," Shane told him. Connor rolled his eyes.

"You're just helping prove my point. I'm helping people. I catch Switchyard, the deaths end. We get paid, Martin and Sarge and the rest live their lives, everyone wins."

"The Endless Night kills people," Shane told him.

"They did," Connor agreed. "And look at them now. West is dead. I heard you locked Finley in his damn vault. These guys are relics. They're idiots. Why would I risk running a business like that? I get a hundred million selling ghosts. What do I care about assassinating the President of some country I can't even find on a map? Or sabotaging some oil company in the Middle East? I don't want that. I just want the money."

"Sounds incredibly noble," Shane said. "Do you have a reason I shouldn't split your head open right now?"

He held the ax between them, but Connor kept his eyes on Shane, ignoring the weapon.

"Plenty of reasons. I read the stuff the group had on you. You're some kind of hero. You're not a psycho."

"Did you ask Randall West what kind of hero I am?"

"You're a soldier. Soldiers can kill without being murderers. You did what you had to do."

"You're not very persuasive, Connor."

"You want Switchyard, too. I can tell. You came here for Martin, but you want that ghost. You want to stop him."

"And?"

"And what? If I hadn't shown up, could you have made it out of that door? If I don't show you the way, can you get out of here? I have maps of this entire area. I have dozens of sightings, all over these tunnels. We narrowed down where he's nesting to an area just a block or so wide. We almost have him. With your help, we will."

"I'm not here to catch a ghost," Shane reminded him. "I'm not helping you catch one, either."

"So what? You let him keep killing Martin's buddies? If you start hunting him now, it'll take you months to find him. I can save you that time."

"I think you're underestimating my skills by assuming I'm as incompetent as you and your men."

"Yeah?" Connor asked. "How'd that cave-in happen?"

Shane watched the other man sit up, making no move to stop him.

"I saw it," Connor said, gesturing to the camera Shane had discovered. "We have them all over. That's how I saw you that first time. I saw the roof fall in on you, cutting you off."

"The ghost is strong," Shane admitted. "Doesn't mean he can't be destroyed."

"No. But he didn't go toe-to-toe with you. You don't know him like

I do. He held back because he's smart. He knows you're a danger, so he kept his distance. He dropped that tunnel like a hunter setting a trap. He won't get within twenty feet of you ever again. Not now, knowing what you can do to him."

"Thanks to you setting him free," Shane added.

"Exactly, thanks to me. He knows I'm trying to catch him, just like everyone else. He knows no one ever has, and it makes him cocky. He went after all the guys I sent for him. He's not afraid; he's mean. Spiteful. So, he'll let me get close. And together, we have the edge no one else has. Not Randall West, not those hunter teams, no one. I have the knowledge, and you have the skill. We can catch him."

Shane dropped the ax head on the ground with a clank and held onto the handle like a walking stick as he bent over, getting into Connor's face.

"You keep ignoring what I'm telling you. I'm not catching him; I'm going to destroy him. And I will not let the Endless Night start again."

"So, you'll kill me? All I'm doing is trying to catch a ghost and sell it. How is that different from your friend James Moran?"

"James never killed anyone," Shane said, growing tired of Connor's twisting of words.

"No one has died at the hands of any of Moran's spirits? That's a lie and you know it."

"They have killed. James hasn't."

"Same," Connor said, holding up his hands. "If my guys could have taken Switchyard, they would have. They died because they couldn't. You know better than anyone that ghosts will kill indiscriminately. That's not on me."

"You're using the homeless as bait," Shane said. Connor shook his head.

"That wasn't my team. Those were West's guys, not mine. I was never anyone in the Endless Night. I did accounting for them, for God's sake. I don't even own a ghost. I don't want to collect them; it's insane. But I saw the dollars. Billions of dollars, Shane. Just in New England. Imagine what people are paying around the world."

"I don't care."

They stared at each other. Blood still flowed, thickly and slowly, from Connor's broken nose.

"Then help me find him at least. I'll try to catch him; you try to destroy him. Whoever wins, wins. It'll end this for both of us, and we can move on to something else."

Shane wanted to punch him in the nose again, maybe knock a few teeth loose. Instead, he sighed. Trying to capture the ghost was stupid. Switchyard was beyond dangerous. But James had his fair share of dangerous ghosts. Shane had some incredibly dangerous spirits in his house. Even Eloise was a danger. It wasn't his place to say that no one had a right to such things.

He had no intention of helping Connor capture the ghost. He would destroy Switchyard as soon as he could. But if Connor had information on how to track him down, it could be helpful.

No one had discovered where the ghost had come from in more than a century. If Shane couldn't get his hands on the spirit, he could find its haunted item. Either way, it would end up destroyed and the problem would be solved. Connor would have no luck capturing Switchyard before Shane destroyed him.

"I will not let you keep him," Shane pointed out.

"I have no intention of letting you destroy him," Connor countered. "But I promise I won't try to kill you. I'm not West. Deal?"

"Fine," Shane said.

Connor held out his hand. Shane stared at it briefly until the other man lowered it.

"Gentleman's agreement, then. I assume you're not planning to kill me, either?"

"I'll break your arms if you make me," Shane explained. Connor grunted.

"Fair enough."

"Let's go find Martin."

## Chapter 13
# Grasping in the Dark

Connor had an incessant need to make small talk. He spoke as though he and Shane were friends. Even with a broken nose, he was undeterred.

"I remember when I first found out about you. There was an expense report from some guy who needed money for miscellaneous gambling expenses at this Iron Tournament thing…"

He looked expectantly at Shane. Shane said nothing.

"Anyway, West had sent him there to scout for new ghosts. We had a whole Iron Tournament file. Anyway, long story short, he filed a report about you and how he wanted to expense a million bucks to hire a team to kidnap you from your room one night. It was very detailed, down to the cost of shoes that wouldn't squeak on tile floor."

"Great," Shane said.

"Point is, he was writing about your fights like he's ringside in Vegas. So, I pulled your other files. Some field agents can't write to save their lives, but other guys got into it. There's stuff back to your parents going missing in your house, and this ghost in a pond, and man… it was a hell of a read."

"Glad I've been entertaining."

"Why do you have to make everything feel so negative? All I'm saying is you've led a cool life and I think we can help each other."

Shane felt the handle of the ax in his hand, solid and cold and powerful. No one would have known if he just took Connor's head clean off. He knew it wasn't a good idea, at least not until he was sure he could escape the tunnels. He probably would not kill the man, but the thoughts were persistent.

"A cool life," Shane repeated. Those were not the words he would have chosen.

"Very cool. The things you've seen and done. Plus, you're a Marine! It's crazy."

"Were your parents rich?" Shane asked, glancing at Connor. He was still young. He had a look about him that made him seem like he should play baseball in a semi-pro league and hit on women with bad pick-up lines.

"What?"

"Did you ever have anything bad happen to you? You seem like someone who stops to watch car accidents."

For a change, Connor had no quick reply. He just looked at Shane, an unreadable expression on his face in the glow of his lantern light.

"Everyone has their story," he said after a moment. Shane had to laugh.

"I'm sure you believe that when you're not salivating over murder victims and ghosts that tear people to pieces."

"I'm helping people even if you don't want to believe it. You want to be a martyr, and that's awesome for you. You're such a tough guy, such an 1980s action hero. You always have to struggle. Good for you, Rambo. You save lives at the cost of your fingers, your friends, and the woman you love. I want to save lives and get stinking rich. You're not better than me."

"If you're implying you're some kind of hero—"

"No," Connor said, cutting him off. "I'm saying that I can save people's lives. It's a fact. If I have a ghost sealed in a box, that ghost isn't killing Martin or Sarge or anyone else."

"Sure," Shane agreed. Connor was heated now, angry beyond what seemed reasonable. He had touched a nerve.

"If I can sell that ghost to a billionaire in Malaysia and make more money in one afternoon than most people will see in their lives, that's my business. It's not wrong. It's not bad. It's me getting what I can. Better than selling oil or coal. Better than polluting the oceans or exploiting workers for pennies. You're just pissed because you think this is your thing. You're the ghost hunter, and you want to carry that burden alone."

Shane had to laugh.

Connor replied with a childish, mocking laugh. "You think I'm wrong?"

"I think you'll say whatever makes you feel better," Shane said. "And I don't care."

"If you didn't care, you'd help me catch Switchyard."

"No, I wouldn't."

Connor scoffed. His nose had started bleeding again, and the lower half of his face was coated in a smeared, uneven layer of blood.

"Why not?"

"You want to capture ghosts that read people's magazines in the park? Be my guest. This one tried to pull my face off, so he doesn't get a free pass. He drags people into the shadows. He'll keep doing that any chance he gets. Ghosts aren't monkeys you can snatch in the wild and cage in a mansion. They'll get out eventually, and when they do, they're angrier than when they went in, and they have no reason not to kill anyone and everyone they see."

"You don't know that," Connor said.

"I don't need to eat rotten meat to know I won't like the taste. It's a solid guess."

They walked in silence for a long while. The distant rumbling of trains grew louder the closer they got to the new tunnels.

It was getting late, and Shane wanted to find Martin to get him to agree to something. Whatever the man's problems were, Shane wanted him out of the way, at least until Switchyard was taken care of. He considered calling Big Bear but decided against it.

Sick or not, Martin was an adult. He still seemed competent, he just wasn't dealing with what happened to him very well. Shane understood that. The man needed time to get himself together. All Shane had to do was make sure Martin stayed alive to make that happen. He'd destroy Switchyard and be done with it all.

Connor represented a problem that still had no solution. If Shane took the man at his word—something he would not do—then Connor was just an opportunist. He had a way to make money, and he wanted to exploit it. Was it so different from James?

James would never have gone about things the way Connor was, but that didn't matter. The real problem was how much Shane could trust what he was being told. The Endless Night were not just greedy, they were dangerous. If Connor wanted to start that again, Shane would shut him down without a second thought. But he wasn't sure that was Connor's goal.

Selling ghosts for obscene prices seemed offensive for reasons Shane had trouble articulating. But the last thing he needed was the stress of trying to police the motives and morality of people he didn't know. There were plenty of worse things in the world. He didn't want to be involved. If it didn't concern him, he had no plans to stick his nose in. Time would have to tell.

He was willing to work with Connor to find Switchyard. He would work with him and watch him as closely as he could. When the job was done, then he'd decide. And if Connor didn't like it, well, he had plenty more bones to break.

The path ahead of them was ending, Shane could see the wall in the beam of his flashlight. There was a small alcove to the right, some kind of maintenance bay from the looks of things, and another door. Connor led them to it, taking the lead into a narrow hallway to their right.

"These were built for the workers. They were down here for weeks at a time, setting up the tunnels. Process was a lot slower in the 1800s, so the workers had these little bunkhouses set up here and there," he explained.

They passed a small room that must have served as a chapel, in which three rows of benches faced a wall, an ancient cross still hanging above them. Next, was a larger room with the fractured remains of a few bunk beds and what would have been a small kitchen, and then another hole busted through a wall into a tunnel that Connor climbed through.

Shane followed into the colder tunnel. This was a newer section than where Switchyard had trapped him. There was trash and remnants of civilization, and it had a familiar quality. He couldn't say he could tell one tunnel from another, but it looked like the one in which he'd first been attacked by the ghost.

"That way?" Shane asked, pointing the flashlight to the right.

"That way," Connor confirmed.

They continued in silence for a short distance when Shane looked over at the other man.

"What if he comes after you?" he asked.

"Who?"

"The ghost," Shane replied. "You're down here with an ax and a rebar. You have no proper weapons to fight a ghost."

"Risk versus reward," Connor said again without looking at Shane. No punchline followed to show it was a joke. He was serious.

"You would have died, and it just would have been part of business?"

"People who play it safe never make a big score. You don't discover America by sticking to familiar waters."

"Jesus, you're Christopher Columbus now?"

"Columbus. Henry Ford. The Wright Brothers. Neil Armstrong. Whatever. Make fun if you like, but I'm trying to run where other people crawl."

"You need to run your ass to a doctor for some pills to help with your delusions," Shane told him. Connor laughed at that, and Shane shook his head. If Connor was lying, he was doing a good job, which more than likely meant he was just that reckless.

Shane had met people who did foolish things for money. It was the standard for everyone in the Endless Night. But he had to hand it to Connor. While the others were willing to let other people die, they didn't seem to want to partake in the danger themselves. Connor was a different kind of idiot.

"You don't think you're at risk, do you?" Shane asked. Connor looked at him, confused.

"I just told you I'm here to take the risk."

"You said that, yeah. But I don't think you believe it. You think you're taking risks in the way a skydiver does. It's a rush, but you have that chute. No one jumps out of a plane expecting to die. You don't think Switchyard is going to kill you."

"I don't plan to let him, no," he said.

"What do you mean?"

"Who plans to fail?"

Again, no punchline. Connor expected to live because dying didn't fit his plans.

*It's a stunning way to conduct business*, Shane thought.

If he didn't kill Connor, the man was still courting a very short lifespan. There had to be something the Endless Night taught each other, some secret they all believed based on lies about just how dangerous the dead were.

They made it to the storm sewer entrance with no sign of the ghost or anyone else. The unpleasant smell was as strong as ever as they trudged through the muck and made their way back to the camp platform. The sun had set, so the limited light that filtered into the tunnel was gone. The place was as black as everywhere else.

"Something's wrong," Connor pointed out as they approached.

There were no voices from the small camp, no fires burning, or small lanterns lit. Connor pulled himself onto the platform and moved for the nearest tent, pulling aside the flap. The soft white light from the lantern he held filled the emptiness. A rumpled sleeping bag, a nearly flattened pillow, and bundles of clothing. No sign of the occupant.

Shane made his way to Martin's tent. He ignored the others and kept the beam of his flashlight on target. A smudge on the concrete caught his attention. Nothing large, but still noticeable. A smear, just a few inches long.

He approached it carefully, listening for any sounds, feeling the flow of air on his flesh. Three dark red, equally spaced lines spanned a few inches across the concrete floor. Blood, trailed by three fingers trying to grab hold of something, in the dark.

## Chapter 14

# Traps

Shane crouched, touching the edge of one of the bloody streaks. It was cold but tacky. It had not been there long enough to dry.

"Shane," Connor called out. He turned back and saw the other man standing at the edge of the tent nearest the fire barrel. Connor held the tent flap in one hand and the lantern in the other. Beneath it, Sergeant Hamlin's head lay motionless, the eyes missing and his mouth still open in what looked like a silent scream.

"There's no body," Connor said. "Barely any blood, either."

"I got blood," Shane said. The streaks were intentional. Switchyard didn't have to make a mess when he killed. He left them on purpose. He didn't need to leave the head, either. He could have taken them to whatever secret place he'd stashed his victims' over the years. The place Connor hadn't found. The place any of the Endless Night hadn't found.

Shane was sure the blood was Martin's. There was no sign of any other dead on the platform. But they were the only two, besides Connor, Shane had spoken to.

The ghost was observant. Cautious, and well-hidden. He had watched Shane on the platform and waited for his chance. He would have known about Connor's cameras. Maybe he had trapped Shane where he did on purpose, knowing Connor would go looking for him. He wanted them out of the way long enough to clear the platform.

"Fingers," Connor said, coming to Shane's side and looking at the blood streaks. "You think it's Martin?"

"Pretty sure," he replied.

"Is this a threat or a punishment?"

Shane looked at the other man, considering the question.

"Maybe both."

It was out of character for Switchyard to attack so aggressively, Shane thought. Based on what he'd heard, the ghost was more opportunistic. He hunted like an animal, but this was him switching back to the calculating mind of a human, not a beast. This was cruel, a lesson for Shane and Connor, and a show of strength and strategy. This was Switchyard saying he held the cards, and they were on his turf.

"Why has no one ever smelled anything?" Shane asked suddenly. The thought struck him as if from nowhere.

"What the hell does that mean?" Connor asked.

"He has bodies. Dead bodies smell. You have his space narrowed down, you said. How come there's no smell?"

Connor stared at him. Shane could see the gears working, the man trying to figure something out.

"Has to be… something with ventilation? Or well-sealed," he suggested.

"What would fit the description of the space you already know about?"

"If I knew that, I would have looked there already," Connor replied.

"It's obviously not a place you know. So, what don't you know? You've mapped this place, right? Where on a map do you have a gap where nothing should be?"

"Nowhere," the other man said. "I know how maps work."

"No, you don't," Shane told him. "If you did, you'd know where to look. We need to look at a place you've already decided is nothing. Somewhere with hidden space. Tunnels no one here knows about. Hidden rooms, spaces under things. Or above them."

"I have guys that can help with that."

"Guys?" Shane asked. Connor nodded, pulling out a phone. Shane shook his head, reaching for it as the other man pulled his hand away, holding it up. The screen was illuminated, and Shane could see a text had been sent to some recipient already.

"What did you just do?"

"Messaged my people," Connor answered. "If you want to know what happened to Martin, we have to do this my way."

"No, we don't," Shane countered. "I've never needed a partner to get the job done in the past. I don't need one now."

"Yeah? How many people had died when you flew solo missions?"

Shane's hand was on Connor's neck in an instant, and he pinned him to the wall, putting just enough pressure on his throat to make him choke.

Connor struggled in vain, but he was shorter and weaker than Shane, and caught by surprise.

"How about we add one more?" Shane suggested.

"You're a fool if you don't accept my help," Connor gasped.

Shane pushed harder but did not reply.

"What if Martin is still alive? You're willing to get him killed to spite me?" Connor's face was flushed red and he struggled to breathe, holding Shane's wrist with one hand and clasping his phone with the other.

Shane relented, letting him go but keeping his eyes locked on the smaller man's.

"We don't need your people."

"You don't know my guys," Connor argued, rubbing his throat and coughing. "They're good at what they do."

"Then who were the guys you sent in who died? Guys who aren't good at what they do?"

"It's a process," Connor explained. "It takes time to learn your enemy and build a team primed to hunt it."

"Of course."

"Give me time. I'll check the camera footage from everywhere, get my team up to speed and geared up. We'll be back and on Martin's trail before you know it."

Shane said nothing and Connor held up his phone again.

"I already sent the message to get the ball rolling. If I don't turn up, they'll come looking. And they're not going to be looking to ask questions first."

"Do what you want," Shane told him.

"We won't be long. You can wait here and—"

"I'm not waiting for you. Come back or don't, I don't care."

Connor sighed loudly, pausing before speaking again.

"You should wait. You don't know where to go, you—"

"Clock's ticking," Shane interrupted. He turned his back and started walking to the far end of the platform. He doubted Switchyard had left any additional clues for him to suss out, but the ghost could have overlooked something.

Connor muttered something Shane couldn't make out. He would be back in less than an hour, Shane was positive. He didn't care, because he wasn't planning on joining his team. Connor needed to get that into his head.

Shane inspected the tent with Hamlin's head inside. There was minimal blood spilled. For a kill of that magnitude, the interior should have been awash in it. You can't remove the head of a living man without spilling a lot of blood. There were only drops, maybe less than half a cup from what Shane could see. The kill had to have been very meticulous. No rushing that one, however it had gone down.

It was unnecessary to kill Hamlin the way he had, but he had done so anyway. He put himself at risk of discovery by doing something like that. It spoke to the ghost's confidence. He had no genuine fear of reprisal. Few ghosts did, of course. But this one usually hunted like he did. So, what was the difference now?

Shane looked at the dead man's head. With its missing eyes and mouth agape, it was a vision of horror. A nightmare, something that would scare most people off and haunt them for life. But not Shane. Not Connor. Not people who hunted ghosts.

What Switchyard had done to Hamlin was meant to enrage. It was a tease. A dare.

Like the ghost was saying, "Look what I can do. Catch me if you can."

Switchyard wanted them to come looking. He let them know he had killed Hamlin outright but Connor was right. There was a chance Martin was still alive. Switchyard baited a trap and was waiting for Shane to fall into it.

He turned to look back, shining his light toward the tunnel that led to the storm drain exit. There was no sign of Connor and no sounds coming from that direction.

Shane wondered how smart Connor was. He had long considered the Endless Night idiots. Connor played the part well enough. He was the accountant of the idiots, at least according to himself. Just a naïve, low-ranking pencil-pusher who found a way to make it big. But what if he wasn't?

Connor said he'd read up on Shane. The Endless Night had an infuriating level of intimate knowledge about Shane's personal life and past. He had no reason to doubt Connor had lied about that part. Maybe he even knew Shane better than he'd let on.

Shane didn't like the idea of being manipulated or playing into anyone's hand. But he still felt like something didn't smell right. Something about Connor was off. Something about the whole situation was.

*Bait*, Shane thought. *They use people as bait.*

The homeless had been easy bait. Something to slake the ghost's thirst for killing, but that was just like providing bread and water to a prisoner. It was sustenance, but it wasn't fulfilling.

Switchyard's collapse of the tunnel showed intelligence and critical thinking. He had slaughtered a man and spilled almost no blood. That was not an act of panic or a lack of control.

Switchyard was excited. He knew Shane could hurt him. That was something he had probably never experienced. So, while he was cautious enough to keep his distance, to drop an entire tunnel ceiling between himself and Shane, it wasn't an act of fear. It was strategy.

If Switchyard were a big game hunter, the homeless would be like goats tied out for him. Boring and unfulfilling. Shane was something different. A lion that could attack. A thrill.

Shane turned, flashing the glow of his light around the platform, looking over the tents and ramshackle structures. He saw nothing.

He raised the flashlight after a brief pause, scanning the corners and overhead beams until a glint caught his attention. Another small, black camera was set up to observe the platform. Connor's spy equipment.

Shane was the bait. He was what Switchyard wanted. He was new and dangerous and thrilling. And Connor knew that.

He made his way back to Martin's tent and pulled out the sleeping bag. A train's brakes squealed nearby. Shane folded the sleeping bag in half and tossed it to the ground next to the wall before sitting on it. His gut told him it was time to do something unexpected. It was time to do nothing.

The stone wall was cold against Shane's back. He pulled a cigarette from his pack and raised it to his lips, holding it there for a moment. Martin was at risk, he knew that. But he was being played. The more he thought about it, the more certain he was. Connor and Switchyard wanted Shane to do this alone. They wanted him in the tunnels, hunting. It was a gamble, and he was playing with Martin's life, but he had a hunch he needed to follow.

Shane lit the cigarette. Brakes squealed again, and he glanced up in the darkness toward the camera he'd seen.

*Who's watching?* he wondered. *Connor, or one of his "guys"?*

It didn't matter.

Shane smoked and sat in the dark. He listened to rumbles and rattles and squeals. Trains came and went. He could even hear distant horn honks sometimes, from traffic up above, filtering down through the storm drain tunnels.

The sharp, metallic cry of brakes rose again, piercing through the walls and growing in intensity. The train was closer than any Shane had heard.

He inhaled deeply, holding the smoke as the shrill sound grew louder. Tendrils of smoke crept from his nostrils. The brake sound lost its metallic trill and became more nuanced, more organic.

Shane exhaled. It was no longer the sound of brakes but of screams. Panicked screams of terror and pain. They echoed along the tunnel even as the cold crept across Shane's legs where he sat.

The darkness around him felt like it was thickening. It coagulated and swallowed the faint sense of shape and structure his eyes had adjusted to.

A scream pierced through it only a few feet away, near Hamlin's tent. It was the older man's voice, the cry coming out wet and ragged until finally, it was smothered by bubbles and gurgling, the sound of a man drowning in his own blood.

Shane exhaled, blowing smoke toward the sound.

"Not a lot of patience for a hundred-year-old ghost," he said to the darkness.

He pointed the flashlight to his right. The camp was gone. The platform was gone. He was surrounded in darkness as thick as mud, the smoke from his cigarette and a dense, gray mist swirling in the beam making it look like the dark was dancing all around.

He was sure Switchyard was there somewhere. Shane stayed seated.

"Shane!" a voice cried in the dark. Then another. And another. Men and women, near and far, called out in panic. Some whispered in shuddering voices, others shrieked as though they were in the final throes of death.

He drew in another lungful of smoke and exhaled calmly. Shadows and voices were amateur-hour tactics. He would not rise to the bait.

"Shane, help me!" Martin cried out. The voice was close, enough to give him pause and flash the beam toward the source. He saw only the darkness.

"He's going to kill me!"

Shane grunted and lowered the light. He rolled the cigarette between his fingers. It would be unwise to show no caution, to let his guard down fully. But he had no plans to move. Not yet.

The voices and screams ended abruptly. The platform went silent once more. Shane could see the vague outline of shapes in the dark again. He flashed the light around him, looking over the support pillars, the brick walls, and the tents of the camp. Everything was as it had been. He stayed seated.

Seconds ticked by while Shane waited for something. He could not say what it might be, but he had no doubt the ghost was not done.

The rattling of a distant train was the only sound now. No screams, no voices. Seconds became minutes and as the rattle continued, the steady beat of wheels on tracks, he saw something in the distance. A single pinprick of light, directly ahead of him.

And it was coming closer.

## Chapter 15
# Death Squad

The walls had begun to vibrate. Shane got to his feet as the light grew in intensity, blinding him as he looked forward. The world had changed, and he was no longer against the wall on the platform, he was standing in a tunnel, his feet planted firmly between the rails.

Dust fell in tiny bursts as the train thundered down the tracks toward him.

"I can't open it!" a familiar voice yelled. Shane turned his head and looked at the door next to him, the new lock reflecting the lights that lined the walls of the tunnel.

"Jaker?" he asked. The lights flickered, and the train rumbled onward. The headlights had bathed him head to toe in yellow. The sound of steel wheels on the tracks was so loud, he could barely concentrate.

The ghost on the other side of the door yelled, but the words were swallowed by the train's rumble. Shane moved to the door, pounding his fist against it. It was cold and rough from the flaked paint and years of rust. He slammed against it and the hinges held fast. The train grew ever closer.

"Shane!" Jaker screamed, muffled behind the door. The train headlights were all he could see now.

"Get down! Fast!" the ghost advised. It was his only hope. He'd have to dive for the tracks and hope the train passed above him. There was no place else to go.

The space between the rails was narrow. The clearance would be barely anything. Shane wiped the sweat from his face as he prepared to dive and flatten himself, then winced as a flash of pain ran up his hand. He looked at his palm, and the tiny burn that still stung him just above the wrist, dirty with dark ash.

He touched his face and pulled the cigarette from his mouth.

When the hell did he light that?

The train was roaring like a living thing. It should have hit him already, shouldn't it? It was only seconds away.

He stood his ground. The light blinded him, the floor vibrated as though an earthquake were shaking the tunnel and the sound was nearly deafening. It all just kept going.

Shane squeezed something in his grip and looked down. Flashlight. He raised it, pointing the beam at the train. Or what he had thought was a train. There was nothing there. He was standing on Martin's platform.

Jaker and the tunnel had been hours ago. He flashed the light at the floor and stared down at the fire ax, the rear spike wedged into a crack in the cement, the blade facing up. Right where he planned to dive to escape the train.

Switchyard was good. Craftier than he'd thought. It had been a long while since a ghost had created something so realistic that Shane had fallen for it, even if only for a moment. A moment pulled from his recent past. He'd been watching Shane even then.

He bent down and pulled the ax from the cracked pavement. He would have fallen face-first on the blade if he'd followed through. Split his head right open to escape a train that wasn't there.

Then something clattered in the tunnel's darkness ahead of him and to the left. He grasped the ax and turned the flashlight toward the sound. Metal rustled and clicked. Multiple gun barrels were pointed at him. Six armed men stood in the tunnel, with the seventh still at the break in the wall that led to the storm sewer exit. A ghost was with them, a tall, slender woman with silver hair and lips as red as blood.

The ghost smiled but the others, dressed in full tactical gear, remained frozen with their automatic weapons trained on Shane.

"Easy now," Connor said, separating himself from the pack. The others were slow to respond. "He's with us."

The men dropped their guns, though none of them looked thrilled.

"You waited," Connor said, surprised.

"Looks like it." Shane checked his watch. Nearly forty minutes had passed. It had not seemed that long. Switchyard had put in the effort to trick him. He could have tried an outright face-to-face attack again, but he was trying a new ploy. He was testing Shane's limits. The direct attack had failed, and the illusion had failed. If he had other tricks, then he would roll them out soon, Shane knew.

"This is the team I assembled to track down Switchyard. If we can't all do it together, it can't be done," Connor said, gesturing to those he brought with him as they climbed onto the platform.

"This is Rigg, Hamish, Tooms, Akerman, Yanish, and Pulaski. They're the best of the best."

"I bet," Shane said. The nearest of the group, and the oldest, scowled openly. He had a tag on his jacket that said Rigg, and Shane snickered.

"Something funny?" the man asked.

"Covert team with name tags," he answered. "Nice touch."

Rigg appeared close to Shane's age, while the others were much younger, all in their twenties from the looks of them. They carried themselves like soldiers, but ones who had yet to be tested. Ones who hadn't lost a fight yet.

"Laugh while you can," Rigg said. "We'll see who's got a smile on their face when this is over."

Shane looked the man up and down. He wasn't familiar at all, but his attitude seemed to be something beyond standard bravado. He seemed like he hated Shane.

"I piss in your cornflakes or something?" Shane asked.

"No. You just killed some of my friends. Broadbent, Sykes, and Mitchum," he answered.

"Not ringing a bell," Shane replied.

"They were tracking you in a swamp down in Louisiana. None of them made it back."

"Oh… those guys," Shane said, nodding. "Didn't have time to ask for their names."

Rigg's arm tensed, and he looked ready to raise his weapon before Connor laid a hand on his shoulder.

"Part of doing business," he said, more to Rigg than Shane. "If you guys aren't prepared to die, you're not in the right field of work."

"Unless you're already dead," Shane added, nodding to the ghost. She was hanging around in the background behind the others, drifting in and out of sight. Her eyes remained locked on Shane, pale and lifeless though they were.

"That's Val," Connor explained. "She has a knack for spotting stuff the rest of us can't. Took me weeks to get her here."

"I like it here," the ghost said, her voice soft and breathy. "I like the dark."

"She's strange," Connor added. "But she has great reviews."

*Great reviews*, Shane thought. The man was acting like this was a food-delivery gig. Or maybe he was still playing the idiot role. Maybe he'd brought a mercenary who wanted to kill Shane and had reason to hate him entirely by coincidence. Anything was possible.

"You got special ghost bullets in those guns?" Shane asked. Connor seemed surprised by the question.

"We come prepared for anything," Rigg answered.

"You've come prepared for ghosts who need to be shot? Huh. That's outside-the-box thinking."

"Didn't say anything about ghosts," the mercenary countered. Shane smiled.

"Mr. Rigg, if I didn't know better, I'd think you were threatening me. You know how much of a mistake that would be."

"Guys, come on," Connor interrupted. Rigg ignored him.

"Mistake? How's that?"

Shane shrugged, lighting a new cigarette.

"I don't know. Ask your buddies Broadway, Spikes, and Swamp Gas."

Rigg made his move, leaving his gun strapped at his side but raising a hunting knife. Shane had the blade of the ax pressed to the side of the other man's face before he closed the gap. Both stood frozen.

"Whoa!" Connor yelled, not quite putting himself between them. "This is not getting the job done. We have a million-dollar ghost on the run here; let's focus on that, okay?"

He reached slowly for Rigg's arm, lowering it and the knife that was still nowhere near enough to be a danger.

Shane grinned, the cigarette dangling from his lips.

"Listen to Junior, Rigg. You can't cash your fat mercenary paycheck if I bust your head open like an egg."

"I like him," Val said from the rear of the group. "He's funny."

"Real riot," Connor agreed. Rigg re-sheathed his knife as Shane pulled the ax away.

"I love a group dynamic," the mercenary said. "So many exciting personalities."

"We need a team to get this done," Connor said. "I'm not letting Switchyard get away again."

"He's baiting us," Shane pointed out. "Not that you aren't aware of that. We need to worry more about us surviving him than him escaping."

"You scared?" Rigg asked. "Kid here talked you up like you were the devil himself."

Shane glanced at Connor, who shrugged.

"Just trying to make sure everyone knows the score."

"I know the score," Rigg replied. "Let's get moving. It's starting to stink down here."

He turned his back and made his way to the platform edge, the rest of his team following. Shane had to laugh again. His departing statement sounded like an '80s action movie line.

Only Connor and Val stayed on the platform with Shane.

"Here," Connor said, handing Shane a backpack. "Got a lead-lined box in there, and some iron."

Shane dropped it to the ground and frowned.

"No," he said.

The other man sighed.

"Fine. Whatever. Let's just get going. And try to leave Rigg alone, alright? He will kill you if you push him."

"Thanks for bringing him along," Shane replied, exhaling a puff of smoke. He turned his attention to the ghost. "What about you? Got plans to kill me?"

"I'm just here to find a ghost," she replied.

"Good enough. I'm with her."

Val smiled, her lips parting over teeth that were stained red. Tiny bubbles of blood popped about in her mouth. Shane hopped off the edge of the platform and the ghost followed him down, with Connor bringing up the rear.

"Just keep up. I caught some stuff on camera before Switchyard disabled a few," Connor pointed out, passing them to catch up with Rigg and the others. Shane looked up at the platform camera.

"Lead the way," he said.

They made their way back to the stinking storm drain and into the abandoned tunnels once more, the mercenaries using gadgets like night vision and motion detectors as they scanned the path ahead.

"I heard this ghost is impossible to find," Val whispered to Shane as they held back from the others.

"He's been a troublemaker," Shane said.

"He's killed many people?"

"Seems like it."

"Do you want to sell him for money?" Val asked. Shane looked her in the eye. They were cloudy and unfocused like she was not even looking at him.

"I want to destroy him and then go get a cup of coffee."

Val's bloody smile spread wide.

"Your name is Shane?" she asked. He nodded. "I like you."

"Swell," he replied.

Rigg turned on a bright light at the head of the group and scanned the tunnel floor. The beam was a vibrant violet shade, and he swept the ground with it until he caught sight of something that drew his attention.

"Blood trail," he shouted. The others refocused on him and took positions flanking and watching his rear.

"Death is waiting," Val said.

Shane nodded and headed after the others. *It is, indeed.*

## Chapter 16
# Awaiting Death

The blood trail went cold at the place where Shane had first encountered Switchyard. The massive splatters on the wall, long since dried, marked the last place the team's advanced blood-tracking light could detect anything. Rigg went ahead several yards and found nothing else anywhere. The ghost had cleaned up after itself as it had on the platform with Hamlin.

"He left the trail on purpose, I bet," one of the men suggested. "We should double back."

"No," Connor said. "This is the sweet spot. Trails don't matter. He can only go so far from his home base. That's what we're looking for."

"How'd the blood trail just disappear?" another asked. Someone snorted.

"He's a ghost, idiot. He can walk through walls."

"So, what's on the other side of the wall?"

No one answered and the man—Shane thought he might have been called Akerman—nodded, and pulled out a brick of plastic explosive from a pocket in his vest.

"Let's blow a hole in the wall and see what's behind it."

"And collapse half of Boston on our heads? No thanks," Rigg replied. He wasn't helplessly stupid; Shane was glad to see that. On the other hand, Akerman was, and someone had given the man bricks of explosives.

"Look here," Connor suggested, pulling out a tablet computer and opening a map. It was a simple layout of the tunnels, and he used his fingers to adjust the orientation and zoom.

"This is where we are right now," he said, pointing at a blank spot. "This place is all mapped out, but somewhere in here is where Switchyard has to be."

The section on the map was a large green circle that covered too much ground. There were tunnels, walls, and empty spaces with little sign of what any of it was.

"We're going to sweep across, covering this entire circle. You need to inspect every inch of wall, ceiling, and floor in this zone. Look for doors, grates, loose stones, collapses, pipes, I don't care what. Anything that could hide a space where this ghost could be."

"He's a ghost, though. Couldn't his haunted thing be anything? A coin in the dirt? An old watch?"

"Yes," Connor answered. "But he's got a person with him, plus every other body that he's killed. He has space somewhere. A platform, a station, a room. Something."

Shane watched the group work while Val puttered about like a bored child. She picked at the blood smears and stared at the ceiling.

Connor had said the ghost was good at whatever she did, which had to involve tracking. The living crew did not have a sense of having worked together as they questioned the map and developed a plan of attack. Rigg began giving out assignments, breaking up the group to follow different paths in pairs. Shane said nothing to disagree with the tactic, though he was certain the team was being set up to fail and probably die. Connor said nothing, either.

"Shane, I'm sticking with you. Which way are we heading?" Connor asked.

Shane looked at the map again. A quarter of the circle was empty space, a void off the first tunnel he'd entered after meeting the male and female ghosts that had told him Switchyard's name.

"Let's go there," he suggested.

"There's nothing there," Rigg pointed out. "You're heading under Boston Common. They never built down there."

"Then it'll be a quick search."

"Waste of time," Rigg grumbled, sending two other teams to search branching tunnels. One led toward the fungal ghost's office. Shane had yet to explore the other.

Rigg took Akerman with him and headed in the same direction as Shane and Connor until they reached the passageway that separated platforms. The mercs continued northward while Shane branched off with Connor and Val.

The passageway led to a station stop that marked the end of the line for some route. One tunnel was walled off, and the other continued west on a curve to the south. Everything north of the tunnel was what Rigg had said was under Boston Common, all empty space on Connor's vague map of where Switchyard had to be hidden.

With only a mile radius to travel from his haunted item, a location under the park wouldn't have been ideal for hunting. The ghost would have had no choice where that item ended up, but this area would have helped keep the item hidden. If no one thought anything was built off that tunnel, then they were less inclined to look there. But that didn't mean there was nothing there.

Connor walked at Shane's side while Val drifted here and there, random things catching then losing her interest. The tunnel did not differ from the others Shane had entered. Lots of stone and dust and not much else. There was no smell beyond the stale scent of old air and mildew.

If the ghost had dragged bodies there, they were still well hidden. The smell of death was hard to mask and hard to mistake for anything else. Shane didn't detect it.

They followed the tunnel into the darkness, with Connor's lantern light illuminating nothing new with each foot they covered. Only a few dozen yards ahead, another platform came into view on the right. It was old, like the one where he'd found the fungal ghost, and it showed no sign of anyone having set up camp there.

"You mapped this?" Shane asked as they approached.

"Yeah. It was another office station, but they ended up switching to the one I found you in before. Administration stuff, mostly."

"But why is it here?" he asked. He turned, pointing his light back the way they'd come. "You can almost see the other station stop from here. Why is this so close?"

"It's older," Val said. She pointed at the bricks. "The color doesn't match. They probably built this first and then changed their minds."

"Yeah, they switched to the other one like I said," Connor added.

"So, what is this, then?" Shane asked.

"Junk," Connor replied. "We searched it already. It's empty."

Shane hopped onto the platform. It looked very similar to where he had been before, down to the green, rusted door.

He took the door by the handle and pushed. It opened with little effort. The lock on this one had been broken and though the hinges were stiff, they still moved. Inside was a hallway identical to the one Shane had seen before, only this time there were no light fixtures or doors in place. The room at the end of the hall, what would have been the bathroom, was unfinished. Just an empty space, like the office to the left.

"This was open when you searched before?" Shane asked. Connor nodded.

"I'm telling you, we looked through here. There's nothing."

"What about the door on the far side?"

"There's just a locker room back there, like a break room or something. This never connected to anything."

"You know something," Val said, interrupting the conversation. She was smiling at Shane.

"Just guessing," he corrected. The ghost held out her hand in the hallway like a child dangling it out of the window of a moving car to surf the air currents.

"Feels cold," she said.

Ghosts could not feel cold, as far as Shane knew, and the air did not feel any colder to him at all. But that wasn't what she meant.

"Switchyard is in a place you've never found," Shane reminded the other man. Connor looked down the hallway at the empty bathroom.

"Yeah," he conceded. "I guess so."

Shane said nothing else. He headed down the hall, glancing into the empty, doorless rooms as he went. There were spots where plans to add fixtures seemed to have been made, but the construction process had not gone that far. He wondered what could have caused them to abandon their plans if they had already committed to building that much office space. The tunnel outside and the platform had seen some use and connected to the older tunnels farther east.

He turned right down the hall away from the bathroom and continued forward. The room at the end of the hall was open, another empty room with missing fixtures. To the left, it was as Connor had said. Instead of another rusted door to a new platform, there was simply a wall of ancient lockers.

Shane approached the room cautiously. He could detect nothing different in the air. No smells, no temperature shifts. Nothing out of the ordinary.

He swept his light through the room. A dozen metal lockers, all unlocked and suffering the ravages of age. Empty spots for overhead lighting. Nothing else.

Shane opened the locker that would have been in front of the exit door. It was just a locker. He opened the next one, the hinges creaking. Another empty locker.

"Told you there's nothing here," Connor said confidently.

Shane grunted, walking down the line of lockers, and opening each one. Val glanced into each one as he went as though assessing its quality. She said nothing, only popped her head inside and looked around before moving to the next one.

"We need to keep moving," Connor told them.

"We do," Shane agreed. He opened the final locker and found nothing but more rusted metal. Val did not follow him to that one. She was still looking in the previous locker.

"You got something?" Shane asked. He returned to the locker she was inspecting and looked inside. The interior was rusted orange with flaking gray paint. He scanned it from top to bottom with the flashlight.

The ghost said nothing, standing to one side. She slipped her hand into the locker, feeling invisible air currents again. Shane looked at her and she grinned, the bubbles of blood making a soft, squishy sound in her mouth.

"What's in there?" Connor asked from behind them both, trying to see inside. Shane reached into his pocket and pulled out the Zippo, flicking the spark wheel as he held the lighter out in the locker. The flame came to life and flickered, swaying slightly this way and that. He held his hand steady, and the flame continued to move.

"Airflow," Connor said. Shane shut the lighter close.

"Airflow," he confirmed. He pushed his hand against the rear of the locker. It buckled and shook.

Val stepped aside as Shane gripped the small coat hook affixed to the rear of the locker and pulled. The panel came away, the rusted edges broken through. Behind it, a hole in the brick wall led to a new tunnel. But it was rough and dug by hand.

Shane directed the flashlight beam into the darkness. Nothing but dirt and rock as far as he could see, and then darkness beyond. It was long, extending to something unseen and unmapped. Something that was not intended to be part of the subway system.

The air did not feel as cold coming up from the tunnel. It hardly moved at all, but it carried something with it. Shane could smell it now, the thing he had been missing everywhere else in the tunnels they had searched. The smell of rot, old and new. The smell of death.

"What the hell is this?"

"This is what's not on your map," Shane answered. "Call your guys."

## Chapter 17
# Somewhere in the Dark

"This is not part of the subway," Akerman noted, staring into the tunnel.

"That's an A-plus for you," Shane remarked.

Rigg insisted on taking point and was ahead of the group. Val followed with Connor, and Shane and the others were behind. He didn't enjoy having Rigg's men at the rear, but he doubted they'd try anything in the tunnel. Not before they had their hands on Switchyard, anyway.

"No, I mean, how did someone build this if it's not part of the subway? And when?" the young merc asked.

Shane had no answer, but it was a reasonable question. The excavation of the tunnel would have been precarious and lengthy. He also couldn't tell if someone had dug through the wall going into the building or out of it.

The path they followed was not a completely straight one. There were dips and rises and slants and curves. The floor beneath their feet was smooth stone. It made Shane think of river rocks, worn smooth over the years of water flow. This tunnel was clear of water or even trace moisture, but it had that same feel. Maybe it had only partially been carved by hand.

"Eyes open," Rigg called back, shutting down more conversation. Ahead, the tunnel widened into a cavern, an open space Shane thought might have also been natural, but it was hard to tell in the poor light.

Rigg stayed ahead of the group, stopping two paces into the new space, while Val slinked along the wall to the right. Connor joined Rigg, but Shane moved to the side with the ghost, as light filled the room and cast shadows at odd angles.

The room seemed to have started as a passage but was chipped away to make it bigger, judging from marks on the stone of the walls.

"We don't want to be here," Val said suddenly, the first time her voice rose. The lights from the crew swept across the room and Shane could see multiple exits leading into more chambers of similar size. There was nothing unusual about any of them he could see at first, but the ghost grabbed his wrist, the cold subdued enough to not be painful but still noticeable to get his attention.

"Look," she said, pointing across the room to everyone's left.

Shane pointed his flashlight where the ghost indicated. He could see something on the ground in the next chamber, a pile of what might have been old fabric and bone. Standing over it was the ghost of a man, the skin removed from his body. He glistened like fresh meat, blood trickling across the exposed muscle. His lidless eyes were focused on Shane and his lipless face exposed a mouthful of shattered or missing teeth.

Because the spirit was devoid of skin, it was hard to judge its expression, but it was not one Shane found pleasant. The ghost raised a bloodied finger to its mouth. There were no lips to finish the gesture, but the sound came through plainly enough.

"Shhhh."

The ghost was gone in an instant, vanished from the light. Val released Shane's wrist and gestured to the other chambers.

"Every room," she whispered. "They're in every room."

The ghost was not Switchyard; that much was clear. Shane moved his flashlight beam to the entrance of the next room, and the one after. He could see into three chambers from where he was standing, but those connected to more. There was something in the center of each, an object, a bone, or something too small to identify.

*Haunted objects*, he thought. They had to be. Switchyard had set up a minefield to guard his location. A labyrinth of ghosts working as guard dogs.

"I don't think your guys are geared for this," Shane said. Connor looked over at him.

"For what?"

"We have movement." Rigg looked at some sort of gauge.

"Switchyard?" Connor asked excitedly.

"Multiple movements," the mercenary clarified.

"Use your eyes," Shane warned. "This is a trap."

Lights darted left and right. The ghosts were hidden away, ducked out of sight, but the air rolled in cold from each chamber. Mists of warm air rose from everyone's faces as they breathed.

"He's right," Rigg admitted, backing another step toward the tunnel entrance. "They have us surrounded."

"Who?" Connor demanded.

A ghost shuffled into the room from the chamber dead ahead. Its left leg was broken with the foot facing inward. The body had been stripped and beaten, the torso a patchwork of massive bruises that looked like they had been caused by punches, one so brutal it had caused a rib to break and puncture the skin.

The ghost was a man, but his face was obscured by a plastic bag pulled tightly over it. The outline of a mouth, open as if screaming, was the only visible feature. The plastic was sucked in so far that the outline of each tooth was clear.

"The hell are we supposed to do here?" Akerman asked. The ghost stumbled closer, his footing uneven on the broken leg and his arms spasming with each step.

Behind the plastic, the ghost groaned. The sound wasn't loud, and it didn't seem to indicate pain or an attempt to communicate. It was just a constant noise, like the thing had been set to go off and it couldn't stop itself.

The stumbling, awkward steps brought it closer to the group. Akerman raised his sidearm and fired, the bullet passing through the ghost's head unobstructed and ricocheting off a distant wall.

One of his comrades cursed him out, slapping down his hand and preventing another shot. The shuffling ghost reached out and clamped bruised, broken hands around Akerman's throat.

Shane pushed past the others to reach the man as he struggled to scream, the ghost's hands cutting off all airflow.

"Get that!" Connor yelled, pointing to the object in the chamber the ghost had come from. Rigg made his move for it as Shane reached the spirit, taking hold of one of its wrists and smashing his arm down onto the ghost's elbow.

The arm broke, and the ghost shrieked, releasing Akerman and turning its attention to Shane. He reached out with his good arm, still unsteady on his previously broken leg. Shane pulled him forward and swept his leg, knocking him down before forcing a knee into his back.

Rigg took a lead box from his pack and knelt next to whatever awaited in the other chamber. Shane had no interest in waiting or seeing what the spirit was bound to. He twisted the ghost's head sharply to the left and pulled at the same time while hooking his fingers under its jaw.

The ghost's head pulled free from his body with a groan. The body burst immediately and the force of it knocked Shane back into Akerman while in the next chamber, the haunted object was destroyed as well, causing Rigg to tumble backward.

"What the hell just happened?" one of the others asked.

The soldiers muttered among themselves while Rigg cursed and got to his feet.

"Ryan!" the man yelled, aiming his weapon. Connor stood between them with his hands up.

"Take your shot if you think you have it," Shane told him. Connor pointed at the other man.

"Do not take the shot," he ordered before turning on Shane. "That could have killed him."

"He's fine. It's not that bad."

"We're not even close to done," Val pointed out, coming closer to Shane. She crouched down and inspected his hands, then touched the ground where the ghost had been. "He's just gone."

"You do that again—" Rigg began, returning to the room. But something raced from the left chamber, knocking the lantern from Connor's hold as it did so and killing most of the light.

"Hold that thought," Shane recommended. Val could see in the dark, he was certain. But the ghosts would take out whatever lights they could.

Shane could make out two ghosts, moving fast, going shoulder to shoulder, and destroying lights. Other ghosts gathered at the chamber doorways, watching. Shane saw at least ten before one ghost made it to him, reaching for his flashlight.

He crouched, lowering his center of gravity, and punched as hard as he could as the ghost ran at him. Not expecting to be seen or countered, the ghost ran headlong into the attack. Shane's strike hit the spirit square in the chest.

The ghost was faceless, the front of its skull smashed in. Shane wasted no time and reached for it with both hands and crumpling the busted skull. A second burst of energy knocked him back, where he was caught by Val as something in a nearby chamber exploded.

"Two down," Shane remarked. The second light-destroying ghost had backed off, allowing Rigg a chance to rejoin the others. They only had three working lights between them now, and the temperature was dropping dramatically.

"How do you do that?" Val asked, running her hands through the air where the ghost had been.

"Just talented, I guess," Shane replied. It was not the best time to entertain questions. The only way the others would be of any help now was to do what Rigg had been trying to do. If they could seal away the spirits, they could limit their numbers. But they had to get to the chambers first and avoid the ghosts that remained. He could distract a few on his own; maybe Val could help. But even the two of them couldn't manage so many spirits at the same time.

"Light 'em," Rigg ordered, pulling glow sticks from a pocket in his tactical vest. His team did the same, and the chamber became bathed in an eerie, green glow. They tossed sticks on the ground and into the nearest caverns.

"Where'd they go?" one of the mercs asked, holding out a tool Shane had never seen. It looked like a radiation detector, with a needle bobbing back and forth as the man scanned left to right.

Shane could no longer see any of the ghosts. He kept his back to the wall and Val stayed close by his side. The soldiers stayed in a tight formation, some of them scanning the place with instruments they had likely purchased from Colangelo. He wondered briefly if the vests they wore were the ones infused with holy water.

"Shane?" Connor called out. He was in the middle of the team, not facing Shane, sliding something over his fingers that, in the green glow, looked like brass knuckles only black.

"Nothing here," Shane replied. "We should fall back."

"We're not falling back," Connor countered. "This is where we want to be."

"This is where you're going to die."

"Do your job and no one has to die," Connor shot back.

Movement from the left chamber silenced Shane before he could comment on Connor's presumption. This was not Shane's job, and the man knew it. He'd convinced himself that Shane was part of the team. When they had a moment to breathe, Shane would have to remind him of the facts.

"Did you see it?" Val whispered.

Shane nodded. The ghost had faded into the shadows, backing into the walls of the chamber. If they were not surrounded yet, they would be soon.

The team held its ground, silent and ready for anything that might come at it, though Shane was still unsure how the men planned to fight ghosts with guns. No one spoke, and the silence of the chamber was overwhelming.

"Up," Val said. She was uncomfortably close to Shane now, and the word was like ice in his ear. He looked at the ceiling of the cavern. The green glow was faint, but he could make out movement across the dome of rock, a gentle vibration as though the stone itself was shifting. The vibration rose to a slow, steady clicking, the noise overlapping like a dozen people snapping their fingers.

Something fell from above them, a chunk that Shane thought was a stone. It landed with a plop on Pulaski's back and the mercenary jumped, looking for what had hit him.

A spider roughly the size of a fist scuttled from his shoulders to the small of his back, avoiding his hand as he brushed it away. The green light made it look black and the bulbous, pulsating torso looked damp and glossy.

"Jesus. Hold still," Akerman told him, using the butt of his gun to try and squish it. He pushed hard against Pulaski's back. The other man screamed as the spider sunk legs like tiny knives under the edge of his vest.

Another spider fell on Yanish, and two more hit Rigg. More rained down, hitting the men and the surrounding cave with a hail of scuttling limbs and fat bodies.

Shane caught one on his shoulder, pulling it away and holding it up in the beam of the flashlight. The body felt as cold as ice but was hard and rough like a crab. The creature's face was a melding of human and spider, with multiple, tiny eyes that gleamed in the light and a small, human mouth filled with needle-thin teeth. It shrieked in Shane's grasp, poking at him with sharp legs that pierced his flesh as he squeezed.

They were manifestations of the spirits; not living things, but still deadly. The soldiers broke formation as the clicking of the spiders' legs spread throughout the chamber, swarming everyone.

The remaining flashlights broke. Only the green glowsticks illuminated the space, making everyone look sickly and spectral as they beat at the ghost arachnids.

Someone screamed though Shane didn't know who. Gunfire erupted, echoing through the stone chambers so loudly that it was nearly deafening. Rigg bellowed orders that were lost in the cacophony, and bullets ricocheted off stone walls, shooting sparks as they pinged off one surface and then another.

"Iron core slugs," Val said, ducking behind Shane to shield herself from the attack. He left her behind as he ran to his right and into the next chamber. He had no idea who held the ghost's haunted item, but she could take a hit and come right back. He could not.

He stepped into the room, lit by just a pair of glow sticks in the entranceway, and ducked low against the wall, out of the range of any gunfire. Shots tore through the other chamber, and someone screamed in pain. Shane turned to look back when something cold and damp covered his mouth.

"Shhhh," a voice whispered in his ear.

## Chapter 18
# Bloodlust

Hands came over Shane's face and pulled him backward in the dark. The taste of rotten meat filled his mouth as his head slammed hard into the stone floor. The skinless ghost appeared above him, the pulpy meat of its fleshless form barely visible in the dim light of the glow sticks.

With no eyelids, the ghost's eyes seemed manic as they locked onto Shane's. The lipless jaws parted, and a gush of blood poured out, freezing cold and half-coagulated, covering Shane's face and filling his nose and mouth.

He reached out, trying to grab hold of the spirit, his hands sinking into cold, wet meat that felt like an old sponge. Blood filled Shane's eyes and he could not see what he held, but he ripped at it nonetheless, feeling the muscle come away in his grip and then fade to nothing once it was free.

More shots echoed, now in rapid succession, and men screamed. Shane struggled against the ghost's hold and shook the gelatinous sludge loose from his face so that he could see again. The spirit's hands clawed at his mouth and neck, but devoid of fingernails, they only did limited damage.

Shane growled like an animal and thrust his hands up hard, connecting with the ghost's jaw and forcing its head back. Thrown off balance, it loosened its grip. Shane rolled it toward the wall, pinning it between himself and the stone. His eyes were still gummed up with sludge, but he had blinked away enough to make out the form of his attacker.

The ghost snarled, its voice inhuman and strained. Flashes of light from the adjoining room accompanied the chaos of gunshots. They were wasting their time, even with iron slugs for ammo. They'd be sending the spirits back to their haunted items, but someone had spread those items throughout the rooms from which the ghosts were attacking. At best, they were only knocking the ghosts back several feet.

Shane could say nothing by way of a warning, thanks to the fleshless spirit that was still trying to claw at his face and throat. He had the ghost's head against the cavern wall and used his right hand to punch at the exposed throat, smashing into where its Adam's apple should have been.

The ghost gurgled and writhed and Shane scrambled onto it, wrapping his arm around its neck as he straddled the form, easing it away from the wall until he was on its back, pinning it to the cavern floor.

It wriggled and flopped beneath him, but he had no time to try to finesse his attack. Too many ghosts were attacking and Connor's team didn't stand a chance. They might have been idiots, but even idiots didn't deserve to be torn apart by ghost spiders in a cave.

Shane pulled his arm free and pressed down on the ghost's head with both hands. It struggled, and cold, mysterious fluids gushed from its body, covering Shane in a revolting spray of filth.

It was the ghost's last-ditch effort at self-preservation. But it failed.

The spirit's head collapsed inward in Shane's hands. He had only a moment to brace himself for the release of energy that came with its body exploding out with enough force to throw him backward.

He landed hard and groaned as rock bruised his back and legs, but he had no time to deal with it. Bullets peppered the walls of the chamber as another round of automatic gunfire rang out from the adjacent room.

With only the green glow sticks to illuminate the space, it was hard to determine who was who at first. Shane sat up and could see three bodies on the floor of the central room. The survivors had merged into a central group, backs together, trying to fend off the group of ghosts that stalked them.

Bullets ripped through ghost flesh and caused them to vanish, only for them to reappear moments later as they manifested once more.

Val slinked along the shadows, as far from the green light as she could get, tearing apart the ghostly spiders and other things that lurked on the floor when they came close to her or her living companions.

The cavern rumbled, but not with the sound of a train or even an earthquake. A form rose in the center of the group of the living, a ghost larger than any Shane had seen, groaning and rumbling as it split apart the group.

The ghost was nothing more than a shadow, human-shaped but impossibly large, like some Frankenstein's monster hunched over as it pushed the soldiers aside, scattering them to the corners of the room.

With wild panic visible on his face, Akerman spun and fired, scattering bullets across the cavern and shooting two of the others in the process. One of them fell screaming, wounded but not dead, and the others were now yelling for him to stop as they ducked for cover from both the spirits and the friendly fire.

Rigg stumbled into the room with Shane, rolling to hit the ground on his back as he avoided the stray bullets, firing his weapon at the shadow ghost and forcing it to vanish for a moment.

A new ghost swooped into the chamber and landed atop the soldier. It was a woman, short and broad with huge slices in the flesh down her back as though someone had cut away segments of skin.

She laughed and buried her face in Rigg's neck, biting and pulling away a chunk of meat as the man screamed. He clasped a gloved hand to the wound, trying to slow the bleeding, and swung helplessly with the other hand to knock the ghost back.

His defense was useless, and the ghost caught his wrist, holding the arm up with the intention of biting into it as well.

But Shane caught the ghost by surprise. He said nothing and moved swiftly, coming at it from the side and tackling it off Rigg. He took her to the ground and grasped her jaw, jerking it hard to the left while pushing forward with all the strength he could muster.

With his body pinning down the spirit, her neck had no choice but to give way. The flesh didn't feel like a living thing. It was more like cold, stiff putty, and it separated awkwardly. The ghost screamed and Shane grunted, slamming the heel of his palm against her chin. Her neck split and pulled apart as the head released from the body in a second fierce burst of energy that knocked Shane aside once more.

He was less prepared for this blow and landed awkwardly, grunting in pain. The others needed to start restraining the ghosts instead of leaving them for Shane to destroy if any of them hoped to get out alive.

"Stop shooting and start trapping," he yelled, getting back to his feet. His eyes searched the chamber for another target and fell upon Rigg, who had gotten to his feet but was hunched over with a hand on his neck. Blood dripped between his fingers, and he sneered at Shane.

"Giving orders now?" the man asked in a growl.

"Suggestions," Shane corrected. "Assuming anyone wants to live through this."

"I think we're a little past that," Rigg responded. With his free hand, he pulled a gun from a holster at his side. The silver barrel reflected the green light as he pointed the weapon at Shane.

Shane tensed. There were no more than five paces between the two of them, and Rigg could squeeze off a shot long before Shane reached him.

"You sure you're pointing that in the right direction, Rigg?" he asked.

"You're right," the man responded. He raised the barrel slightly, aiming squarely at Shane's head.

"Seems a bit harsh," Shane replied.

"Harsh would be what I planned to do. But I don't have the time to kill you the right way," Rigg said. "This will suffice."

"Kill me and you kill yourself. You think your team will get out of this alive?"

Bullets continued to ring out in the other rooms as the survivors scattered. Shane could only see Connor and Akerman now, but there was muzzle flare in the far chamber. Ghostly screams and taunts echoed through the caverns.

"Already dying," Rigg said. He pulled the hand away from his neck and blood flowed freely. The ghost had bitten deep and torn out a large chunk of his neck. The artery had opened, and blood gushed forth.

"Just enough time… to take you with me."

Two glow sticks near the cavern entrance were the only source of light in the room. Shane's options were limited, and as Rigg spoke, Shane made his move, dropping to the cavern floor and sweeping his leg hard to the left.

The glow sticks scattered back to the room with Connor, plunging Rigg and Shane into darkness. The soldier fired a shot followed by another and another. Shane rolled and scrambled away from the chamber entrance and Rigg, who was desperately moving through the black space and bumbling into rocks and dips in the floor without pausing to try to orient himself.

The sound of shots followed him, but Rigg was as blind as Shane was, and he had no target to aim at. Six rounds fired and Rigg stopped. Shane did as well, not wanting to give the other man any sound to aim at.

"You earned this, Ryan," Rigg wheezed. Shane could not see him but heard some shuffling. Connor had been yelling nearly constantly, as had Akerman and at least one of the others. Ghosts wailed and moaned and growled like beasts. The echo of gunshots reverberated off the walls.

Shane risked giving himself away and moved, circling where he remembered Rigg being, hoping the chaos would cover his tracks. Low to the ground, he scrambled across the room until he had Rigg's silhouette lined up against the glow of the cavern entrance.

Rigg fired again, the bullet hitting the wall on the far side of the room with a flash of sparks. Two more shots and Shane made a break for Rigg just as the mercenary pulled a new glow stick from his vest and cracked it.

Green light sprang to life in his bloodied hand and Shane's face was right there. Rigg yelled, surprised and enraged, dropping the stick and swinging the gun. Shane tackled him, planting his shoulder in the other man's gut and knocking him to the ground.

His focus was on the gun. He took Rigg by the wrist, slamming his hand on the rock again and again to force the man to release his grip. Even in his weakened state, Rigg was strong. He didn't want to let go as he fought with Shane, his teeth gritted and his eyes intense in the eerie glow.

Rigg raged and squeezed the trigger, firing off another shot as Shane wrestled the weapon free. He slammed the man's hand into the rock one more time, and finally, Rigg relented, loosening his grip enough for Shane to pull the gun away.

"I only came here…" he said weakly, as Shane shifted focus, grabbing Rigg by the neck, "…to kill you."

"Should have stayed home," Shane told him, raising his free hand and forming a fist. He paused, ready to strike a blow, his breathing heavy and his heart racing. Rigg looked him in the eye and exhaled. It was a slow, steady release and when he finished, he didn't move again. His eyes stared up. They saw nothing any longer.

Shane released Rigg's neck, warm blood smeared across his fingers. The other man remained motionless.

Gunfire continued in the next room. Someone yelled about being out of ammo. There was no time to waste. Shane left Rigg's corpse, taking the man's backpack and heading toward Connor and the others.

## Chapter 19
# Scorched Earth

A bullet hit the wall behind Shane's head. Stone shrapnel peppered the side of his face and he winced, digging a piece out of his cheek.

"Hold your goddamn fire!" Connor shouted.

Akerman had lost any cool he might have had and was panicking. Yanis, Pulaski, and Hamish were motionless on the ground, and he had taken a gun from one of them, allowing him to fire two-handed. He aimed at anything that moved, popping iron slugs into ghosts.

The iron thrust them back to the haunted items that housed them, but the items were only a stone's throw away. All Akerman was doing was annoying them. When the bullets ran out, he'd die like the rest, if he didn't shoot himself first.

Val was crouched in the tunnel entrance that led back to the abandoned office. She had sunk low to the ground like a snake, watching and waiting for what was to come.

Connor and Tooms were still together in the center of the room, but Akerman had moved off several paces on his own, standing over Pulaski's body. The man was breathing heavily, his face beaded with sweat that reflected the green glow of the light around him, and his eyes wild and unfocused.

"He's lost his mind," Val whispered as Shane circled the room.

The ghosts had fallen back as well, taking refuge in the central chamber that was straight ahead of where Akerman was firing nearly blindly.

"We need to use it while we can," Shane whispered back.

"Run?" Val asked with a grin. He shook his head.

"Trap or destroy," he replied, dumping Rigg's bag. There were only four lead-lined boxes in his pack, and they were small. Depending on what haunted items awaited in the rooms, they wouldn't all be big enough. But they were better than nothing.

Shane threw a box at Connor, trying to avoid Akerman's attention. The box hit him in the leg and he turned, focusing on Shane for the first time since he'd returned to the room. Shane pointed at the box then himself and gestured to the left chamber.

Connor nodded, saying something to Tooms. The men were crouched low, guns ready but avoiding Akerman's erratic fire. Tooms looked back at Shane, blood running down half of his face from a large wound above his eye.

"Come with me," Shane said to Val. The ghost crawled from the tunnel, scuttling along on gangly limbs like an insect, and stuck to his side as he circled the room to Akerman's left and slipped into the chamber.

"What are you doing?" Akerman shouted, catching sight of Shane and the ghost.

"He's trying to save our asses," Connor pointed out. Akerman shook his head.

"There's too many of them. They're gonna kill us. This can't be happening, man. This isn't happening!"

Connor had come to Akerman's side, using the distraction as a chance to get close. He started some kind of inspirational speech but Shane tuned him out, focusing on the empty room ahead.

"There," Val said, pointing at the object in the middle of the cavern. It was half buried in a loose pile of sand and pebbles. It was a watch that Shane thought was perhaps from the eighties.

He ran for it, lead box open, and scooped it up with some of the dirt and stones. He had no idea which ghost had been attached to it and didn't care. Shane closed the clasp on the box and slipped it into the bag over his shoulder.

"There," Val said again, pointing to the far wall. No lights from the glow sticks penetrated that far. All Shane could make out was the entryway, a black void in the stone.

"What is it?" he asked.

"Silver pendant," the ghost replied. "Dead center of the room."

Shane ran to the blackness, a new box open. He felt around with his hands, orienting himself.

"Here," Val said from the dark. The ghost flashed white suddenly, a soft glow in the shadows that made her look terrifying as the light seemed to run through the veins beneath her skin.

It provided little illumination, but it was enough. The light glinted off something small and metallic. A cross, Shane thought, without paying much attention. He scooped it into another box and sealed it.

"We are not alone," the ghost said then. Her light cut off as though a switch was flipped, plunging Shane back into darkness. He froze in place, the sealed box next to him, and listened. Akerman continued to fire, but now, it seemed like he did so more intentionally, working with Tooms and Connor.

Closer to Shane, a clicking sound filled the room. It was like the tapping of fingers on a keyboard and Shane recognized it immediately. The spiders had returned.

"One o'clock," Val's voice said from somewhere far away. "Fast."

Shane grunted, not wanting to trust his fate to a ghost he'd only just met but having few other choices. He adjusted his position slightly and ran into the darkness.

"Low," Val said, closer to him. He balled his hands into fists and bent forward as she flashed with light again. Another doorway to an adjacent chamber came into view, and crouched in it was a spirit covered in the scuttling, clicking bodies of spiders.

Shane dove on the ghost and rolled it over into the next cavern. It was smaller than the others he had fought, its face wizened and sunken, like something had pulled the moisture from it. Its entire body was the same way, little more than a husk.

"Don't fight," a voice whispered close to Shane's ear.

"Don't fight," added another.

"Don't fight. Don't fight. Don't fight."

The ghost he wrestled with said nothing, its dead eyes blind even in the light cast by Val. The voices came not from it but from the spiders it commanded. They spoke with small, human mouths, their voices sounding like hateful whispers.

"He will punish you."

"Don't fight."

"He'll be angry with you."

"He will punish you."

More and more voices joined the chorus, warning and threatening Shane as the spiders swarmed around their master. The ghost was not putting up a fight, but the razor-legged spiders slashed at Shane's hands or face each time he tried to strike a blow or get a grip on the master of the arachnid swarm.

Shane rolled the ghost over against the chamber wall and grasped at its neck, but the spiders slinked from the dark and slashed at his fingers. Thin, papercut-like wounds opened on his hands.

"Val," he growled, swatting away as he felt one scuttle up his back.

His ghost companion pulled the spider off him and crushed it in her hands.

"Traitor," the spiders whispered as one.

"He'll punish you, too."

"He'll be angry."

Val giggled like a child and began stomping on the spiders, crushing them under hand and foot while more coalesced in the shadows to replace them. They were not real; they were just manifestations of the ghost that would never end so long as the ghost remained.

"He'll be angry at you," a spider hissed, climbing onto the wizened ghost's face and looking up at Shane.

"Good," he replied. He grabbed the ghost's head and the spider together and pounded them into the rocky floor of the cavern. The ghost struggled only for a moment while Shane applied pressure until its head caved in and then exploded.

Shane rolled aside, avoiding most of the blowback from the ghost's destruction and saving himself some bruising. The spiders vanished with their master.

"How does it feel like?" Val asked, appearing at his side. Her glow had faded, and they were in pitch darkness once more. Her voice was soft and urgent in his ear. He felt like there was an almost lascivious tone to it like she was trying to sound seductive, which he found more off-putting than the spiders with human faces.

"What does what feel like?" he asked, getting to his feet. The echo of gunshots had slowed considerably. They were targeted shots now, single rounds fired with clear intent.

"Killing the dead."

"Can't kill what's already dead," Shane pointed out.

Something touched his shoulder. Val's hand, gentle but firm.

"Call it whatever you like. How does it feel to end them?"

"Like setting off a grenade in your hands."

She laughed and the dimmest tendrils of light rose through the veins of her face. It looked like a silvery white root system in her skull, concentrating behind her eyes.

"Sounds thrilling," she whispered.

"Next one," he replied, trying to keep her focused. He had destroyed five of the ghosts and captured another two. The problem was, he wasn't sure how many there were to begin with. He was sure he'd seen at least ten. For all he knew, there were a hundred down there. And they had yet to find Switchyard among them.

The ghosts they fought were placed with intention. Haunted items did not find their way to small, strategically placed piles of dirt in the center of linked caverns. The threats of the spiders convinced him that these spirits were, in fact, guardians. Someone had placed them there to protect Switchyard. Maybe they were some of his old victims. Each looked to have died painfully and would likely have fit with Switchyard's style.

It was possible Switchyard held sway over his victims, a kind of hold that transcended death, forcing them to do his bidding even as spirits. Locked in perpetual terror at the hands of the ghost that had killed them. It would have been like waking from a nightmare into a new nightmare that never ended. Or wouldn't have ended without Shane's intervention.

Whether the ghosts were killing for their enjoyment or from fear of what Switchyard might do if they didn't protect him didn't matter much. If Shane couldn't trap them, he'd destroy them all.

He had only come to Boston to help Martin, a man he barely even knew. Things had spiraled out of control at this point, and Shane was now fueled mostly by anger. He was angry with Martin for getting himself into such a dangerous situation. He was angry at Switchyard for what it had done and what it would continue doing. And he felt nothing but rage for Connor and the Endless Night. If not for them, he doubted things would have gotten so bad. Not just in the subway, but everywhere. How many victims would still be alive if not for the Endless Night and their plans?

Val led the way to the next chamber. Shane could see the occasional muzzle flare flashing off the walls from the room where Connor and the others held their ground. The caverns were arranged like a honeycomb around the tunnel through which they'd entered, each chamber connected to at least one other.

The ghosts had pooled together in the central three chambers around where the group had started, leaving the outliers mostly empty. Val led Shane to two more haunted items, filling the four boxes he'd carried with him in Rigg's bag.

"Can you see how many are left?" he asked.

"Just one, I think," she replied. There were two chambers in front of Connor, Tooms, and Akerman. The cavern between them housed the item Shane had prevented Rigg from picking up initially, which belonged to the bag-head ghost he'd destroyed first. So whichever spirit was left was linked to an item he had not seen.

"Connor, you alive?" Shane shouted into the dark.

"Ryan, what's going on?"

"Looks like there's one left. You got a bead on it?"

"No," the man yelled back.

"He's in there, man. He's waiting for us!" Akerman yelled.

"Helpful," Shane replied.

"What do you want to do?" Connor asked.

"Have a smoke and go home."

Val laughed, peering past Shane into the chamber where the final ghost hid.

"Oh," she said. "It's the big one."

Shane cursed under his breath, crouched low, and peered around the edge of the opening. It was the ghost that had risen in the center of the mercenaries during his fight with Rigg, a shadow twice the size of a man. The ghost's head turned as Shane caught sight of it, eyes like burning embers in the darkness locking onto his.

The ghost howled like an animal and broke into a run, thundering across the cavern toward him.

*Damn*, Shane thought, backing away. *This one looks angry.*

## Chapter 20
# Where the Dead Rest

Freezing air blasted Shane with such force that he was pushed backward, deeper into the cavern. The monstrous shadow ghost hit the entrance like a speeding truck and burst through. The dark, frozen air rushed against Shane's body with a sharpness so painful he had to shield his face.

He fell backward, the cold stinging through his flesh and into his skull as though he'd dunked his head in ice water. Connor shouted something, but the words were lost in the roar of the icy wind, like gusts coming alongside an avalanche that threatened to burst his eardrums.

For a moment, Shane laid still on his back, staring up at the dark ceiling faintly illuminated by bursts of green born from the glowsticks the shadow ghost had scattered in its wake.

Darkness swept through the glow, a hand made of shadow. It slammed down square in the center of Shane's chest, pressing his ribs and forcing the air from his lungs. The shadowy hand closed into a fist, gripping Shane's shirt and lifting him from the ground.

Shane struggled briefly, getting a grip on the ghost's wrist, which was so large he could barely grasp it in two hands. Slowly, his flesh sank into the cold substance, finding something more solid within, as though the ghost wore the shadow as armor and his true self was encased inside.

The spirit swung hard and threw Shane across the room. He hit the stone wall with a loud grunt. The force was like being hit by a car, and he collapsed to the floor with a groan, waves of pain rolling across his body.

The ghost thundered toward him again, and a gunshot rang out. The iron slug pierced the shadow body and the spirit vanished, forced back to its haunted item.

"Ryan, you alive?" Connor asked as he entered the chamber with Akerman and Tooms.

"Seems like," Shane replied, his voice strained.

"Where's this ghost's object?"

Shane grunted, getting to his hands and knees. "What?" He needed a moment to catch his breath while he had the chance.

"This shadow ghost. I want him," Connor said.

Shane looked up, and Connor stared back at him expectantly. Tooms and Akerman had their guns at the ready and were nervously scanning the darkness in all directions.

"You're asking me that right now?"

"Have you ever seen one like him? He's massive and powerful. Do you have any idea what he'd be worth?"

"How about a boot in the ass?" Shane suggested. "You want him? Find him on your own."

"He's the last one," Connor pointed out. "It's not going to hurt to trap him."

"When he comes back, let him throw you against the wall."

"You know what I mean. I need something out of this, Ryan."

They stared at each other for a beat that stretched far too long.

"You staying alive is what you get out of this," Shane told him. "If you even get that."

"Don't try to threaten me, Ryan. It's not going to work."

He held out his hand and Shane ignored it, getting to his feet on his own. Val stood behind him, but he ignored her and looked around. The bursts of wind had scattered the glowsticks to random corners. The caverns were dim enough that the shadow ghost could have been anywhere.

"I told you before, I'm not looking to cause trouble. I'm just trying to make a buck," Connor said.

"Or a million," Shane countered.

"Or a hundred million." Connor shrugged. "If I can do it, who cares? I'm not hurting anyone."

Shane raised an eyebrow and glanced in the other man's direction.

"West hurt people. If all I do is sell them, no one needs to get hurt. It's like people with exotic pets. If a rich guy wants to keep tigers and can afford to keep them healthy and safe, who cares?"

"You ever hear those stories about people getting mauled by their pet tigers?" Shane asked.

"One in a million," Connor replied.

"Yeah, one in a million. Except instead of someone sending the tiger to a sanctuary, we're talking about a ghost that can slaughter the whole neighborhood while making the walls bleed and screams come out of the toilets."

"Not my problem," the other man said. "A person could go buy the most expensive sports car today and drive it into a crowd of people. Not the car's fault. People need to be responsible when they own dangerous things. We can't not let people have the option. And that's what you're advocating."

Shane chuckled. He wondered what Carl would think about being compared to a car.

"I'm not seeing this guy anywhere, boss," Akerman interrupted, his gun still at the ready while he scanned the darkness.

"He's here somewhere," Connor assured him. "Val, you see anything?"

"He's right there," the ghost answered, indicating the middle of the room.

Shane followed her line of sight but found it was unnecessary. The shadows formed in the center of Akerman, Tooms, and Connor and coalesced as the ghost rose from the floor again.

Shane backed off. Connor was swift on his feet and ducked away immediately, but his men were less successful. Akerman fell backward and made a move to fire another round but the ghost had already taken hold of Tooms. It held the mercenary like a human shield.

Tooms screamed, wordless fear at first and then in a panic as he saw Akerman's gun raised.

"Don't shoot!" he yelled as the ghost pushed him toward Akerman. Akerman didn't hesitate, firing a single round at first and then another and another as Tooms' body came down on him like a club.

The first shot tore through Tooms' leg, the next his abdomen, and two more hit his vest. Connor yelled for him to stop, but the sound was swallowed in the chorus of panic that had erupted. Tooms shrieked in pain while Akerman shouted in fear. The ghost roared, the sound of a fierce wind howling through the small space.

It was impossible to tell if Tooms was still alive by the time his body slammed into Akerman's. Then the ghost hoisted him and slammed him down once again, crunching his head against the stone and removing any doubt.

Connor raised his weapon and shot the ghost in the side of the head before it could strike any additional blows. The shadow vanished and Tooms' corpse fell in a heap at Akerman's feet.

Akerman's face was a bloody mess, not all of it his. He groaned and rolled over while Connor got to his knees next to the man and hoisted him roughly by his vest.

"If I didn't need you to finish this, I'd put a bullet in your head right now," he said, only the barest hint of emotion in his voice. Akerman sputtered and moaned. Connor slapped him.

"Get up. If you pull that trigger again without my permission, I will leave you down here to rot."

He pushed Akerman back to the ground and stood. Shane was about to offer a sarcastic quip, but he lost the moment as the shadow returned. It rushed through the passageway, coming for Connor this time.

"Down," Shane ordered. The other man did not hesitate or even look confused by the request. He dropped as Shane moved to meet the ghost, going low as well, and aiming for what he hoped was the ghost's knee.

His fist met the joint with only mild resistance. The rushing wind became a howl of pain as the ghost collapsed, the damaged knee down and the other bent to support itself, as Shane had intended.

There was no pause, only the time it took to transition from left knee to right leg. Shane pivoted to the bent knee, placing his left hand atop the shadow ghost's thigh and boosting the leg from under the calf with his right. Off-balance and surprised, the ghost was unprepared and unable to adjust his position. Shane lifted the leg and caused the ghost to fall, giving him more leverage. His right hand forced the shadow limb to its full extension and momentum carried it the rest of the way.

A ghost's leg does not break the same as a living person's leg. The sound was different, as was the feeling. The resistance of ghost flesh was unusual, Shane had learned long ago. It had strength, but it was almost like a strong surface tension. There was no true muscle or bone that needed to be worked through.

The ghost's kneecap buckled, and the leg bent up and back in the wrong direction. The howling wind became a sharp, almost human scream. It happened fast, a quick, sweeping series of actions. Once the knee had broken, Shane hugged the leg around the calf while the ghost fell. He twisted the limb in his grip and spun his body aside. Shadowy flesh tore with minimal resistance. Difficult at first, but once it had started, the rest came apart with ease.

Shane pulled the ghost's leg in half, severing the limb and tossing the stump aside. It fell apart like paper ash in a breeze, becoming nothing before it hit the ground.

The shadows that the ghost had covered itself in like armor drifted away, revealing a smaller, more human-like spirit in its wake. The ghost appeared old, his face that of a wrinkled but brutalized man who looked to have been beaten to death.

"Where is your item?" Connor asked the ghost, approaching him quickly.

"You're all going to die down here," the ghost uttered in a deep, hoarse voice.

"How about you start?" Shane suggested. He moved on the ghost before it had a chance to regroup and adapt to the missing leg.

"Ryan, stop!" Connor shouted.

Shane didn't listen. With one hand on the ghost's throat, he pushed its head aside with the other and crushed it. Connor's protesting yell was overwhelmed by the final burst of a wind-like scream from the spirit. It exploded, throwing Shane back onto the already injured Akerman. He landed and laughed when the man groaned again.

"We could have trapped him," Connor said, coming to Shane's side. "That thing he did? The shadow disguise? That was worth millions."

"Looks like it would have been a waste of money if you ask me."

Connor took a moment, his face betraying his feelings though he kept his mouth shut. Shane got to his feet, straightening his disheveled clothes and brushing himself off. Connor got into his face as he did so, nearly nose to nose as he stared Shane in the eye.

"Switchyard is mine, you understand that? I will not lose him."

"Do your best," Shane replied. "We had a deal, right?"

"I won't try to kill you," Connor said.

Shane smiled. "And I'll do the same."

He didn't trust Connor as far as he could throw the man. Shane was confident their deal was only as good as the advantage it offered in finding and potentially capturing the ghost. When it came down to it, he was certain Connor would try to kill him to keep his prize.

Shane glanced at Val. The ghost smiled at him, that creepy, mysterious smile he was growing used to. She was still a wild card. Connor had brought her for a reason, meaning Shane couldn't rely on her or trust her in a pinch. The potential for a three-on-one fight was not something he relished.

Akerman got to his feet slowly and unsteadily, blood running from his mouth and nose. He felt his chest and didn't straighten up fully, making Shane wonder if he'd broken a rib or sustained other internal injuries. He was another liability. Working for Connor and undisciplined and panicky. All of them were at risk of getting shot by Akerman.

*Four-on-one*, Shane thought. His odds were not good. Of course, they still had to find Switchyard.

"We should just leave, boss," Akerman said, pain clear in his voice. "The whole team is dead. How are we supposed to catch this thing?"

"It's just a ghost. You put his item in a box, and you leave," Connor told him.

Akerman looked at Tooms' body, his blood black in the green glow of the cavern.

"But everyone's dead," he said quietly.

"Then you better do what you can to avoid joining them."

"The only way out is that way," Val said before Akerman could complain any more. She pointed ahead into the dark, through another passageway, and into what looked like another chamber. The light reached no farther.

"Then we go that way." Connor knelt, rolled over Tooms' corpse, and sorted through the man's backpack and vest. He took ammunition and a penlight, turning on the flashlight before hastily attaching it to the shoulder of his vest. The thin beam of white light showed the empty cavern and then another passage into a tunnel like the one through which they'd entered.

"Let's be quick," he said, leading the way. Shane stayed behind as

Akerman hobbled after Connor, retrieving a cigarette from his pack, and lighting it. Val stayed with him, the light from Connor fading quickly.

"Those things will kill you," the ghost said.

Shane looked at her briefly in the light cast by his Zippo. She was uncomfortably close again, smiling at him.

"Can think of worse ways to go," he told her. He imagined he'd see a few worse ones before they were done underground.

## Chapter 21
## Cat and Mouse

Connor moved slowly and unsteadily. The passage was not as easy to travel as the previous one had been. Sometimes, the rock sloped sharply upward or downward and the trio had to drop down or even climb up on hands and knees. Val, of course, had no issues.

The passage wound left and right, serpentine and confusing, but not as long as Shane had expected by the time it opened into something new. The wall was smooth and worn down but not natural as it gave way to a hallway. It was a constructed hall made of brick and stone, albeit narrow and exceptionally old.

Connor's light swept left, and the white beam revealed ancient light fixtures. He approached one as Shane exited the tunnel behind a slow and awkward Akerman, pulling on a tarnished old wall sconce that was covered by a blackened glass cone.

"These are gas," Connor said.

Shane grunted. Boston had used electricity since the late eighteen hundreds, before the creation of the subway system. Wherever they were now predated that.

"Are we still under Boston Common?" Connor asked.

"Hell if I know," Shane replied. He hadn't been sure where they were the entire time; he hadn't spent enough time trying to get oriented below compared to the world above.

"Are we in, like, a basement or something?" Akerman asked, touching one of the walls.

"There's nothing this old in the area," Connor replied. "I mean, there shouldn't be."

"Apparently, there is," Shane pointed out. Wherever they were, it was a place long forgotten over which they had built the rest of Boston. The park was old, he knew that, dating back to the early eighteen hundreds, but there were no large structures in it. There was no reason for there to be a basement or tunnels in the area. At least not one that had made it to the modern world.

"I'm going to have to get another team down here. Who knows what could be hidden away under the city," Connor said, directing the light in the other direction to see what else was around them. The hallway was long, extending a good distance in both directions with the gas-light sconces placed at regular intervals. Aside from thick layers of dust, there was nothing else to see.

"Let's do that on your time," Shane told him.

There was nothing to suggest a direction to continue their search. Connor headed the way he was already facing. Akerman followed closely behind, leaving Shane and Val together once more.

"Do you have any idea where we are?" Shane asked.

"Never been to Boston before," she replied. He recalled Connor saying something about bringing her in from out of town. He still wasn't sure of her specialty or why she was on the team. But with only Akerman left alive, it seemed like no one on the team had a real purpose.

"The air down here isn't stale," he remarked. The ghost's eyes narrowed slightly in the fading light.

"That's unusual, isn't it?"

"Yeah, it is."

Shane started after Connor, not wanting to lose the light or let the other man have a chance to get to Switchyard before he did. The odds of Connor surviving a direct encounter with the ghost seemed slim at best, but Shane was not willing to count anything out.

If Connor was running the show for the Endless Night in New England now, or even just Boston, there was every reason to doubt his story of just being an accountant looking to exploit the ghost-collecting billionaires left in the cult's lower ranks. He had to have another trick or two up his sleeve if he intended to capture Switchyard before Shane destroyed the ghost.

"Shane," Connor shouted from a couple of yards ahead. He had stopped walking and was directing the beam of his flashlight to the right. Akerman had backed against the wall and turned away. He made eye contact with Shane, the panicked expression from his breakdown in the caverns plastered on his face once more.

"Keep your hands off the trigger, huh?" Shane suggested, pushing down the barrel of the merc's gun before looking at whatever had caught their attention.

Val made an unusual humming sound like she was quietly impressed. There was a room off the hallway, the size of a closet, though the door was missing, and the dusty and corroded hinges suggested it had happened long in the past.

There was a body inside the closet. Shane assumed it had been a man based on the coveralls that indicated he was perhaps some kind of maintenance person. The blue material had mostly rotted away where it had not been torn. Beneath it, the body had decayed to little more than a skeleton. The remaining bits of flesh were like tanned hide, leathery and yellowed and stretched across discolored bones except for where the skeleton was broken and crushed in several places.

The skeleton's hands were pinned to the brick wall with rusted spikes. It was on its knees, the feet cut away from the legs and placed neatly beside it, still wearing boots. Throughout the chest and abdomen were a series of other spikes. Large nails and random bits of metal had pierced through it, more than a dozen varying in length and thickness. The killer had planted the largest and thickest through the eye sockets. The skull's jaw hung open which made the man look like an alien head trapped in a perpetual, silent scream.

"Old," Val said.

"For sure," Connor agreed.

"I can see why you want Switchyard so bad," Shane said, inspecting the rest of the room. There was nothing in it and no sign of it having been used for anything else at all.

"What's that mean?" Connor asked.

"He's like you. He likes to collect the dead," Shane explained. "He takes his victims back here. Keeps them. The ones that return as ghosts, he puts out as guard dogs. The rest become trophies."

"What the hell are you talking about, man?" Akerman demanded, his voice shaky. Shane pointed at the pinned skeleton.

"That's what we're dealing with. A ghost who has a fascination with death. I think he just likes watching it happen. Different ways, different reactions. Fits with what we've seen."

Akerman shook his head and scoffed.

"Stupid. That's stupid, man. Those ghosts weren't guard dogs, and this thing isn't some kind of supervillain. Just another spook to box up."

"You think so?" Shane snickered. "All those ghosts placed neat and tidy? He left them there. A little test for anyone who wants in. Booby traps in the front yard."

"That doesn't make sense," the merc replied. "How's he forcing them to do anything? They're dead. They could just leave. They could turn on him any time they wanted."

"They did it because they were afraid not to," Shane answered. It was a guess, but one he felt in his gut. Switchyard had been down here killing for a long time in the forgotten corners of the world below Boston. He'd collected a lot of trophies too, Shane suspected. And those who were unfortunate enough to come back and find themselves in the ghost's grasp even in death were probably too terrified to even think of defying him.

From the perspective of the other ghosts, Switchyard was not just a nightmare who had killed them, he was something that would torture them for the rest of time. He was Hell. And all they could do was try to keep him happy in whatever deranged and violent form that took.

Shane could prove none of it, but the ghosts he had seen lent some strength to the theory. The skinned ghost, the brutally beaten one, the one with broken bones and the bag on its head. Switchyard didn't kill the same way twice. The ghost subjected victim after victim to something new and awful.

Shane wondered how many there could have been. After more than a century? How many people could he have dragged into the dark to a place no one even knew existed?

"We need to keep moving," Connor suggested, looking ahead and ignoring Shane.

The man had focus if nothing else, Shane would give him that. Even in the face of all the death and pain on display, he had not wavered in his desire to capture Switchyard.

They moved as a group away from the corpse, farther down the hallway to a junction. The hallway split left and around a curve, past which Shane could not see. To the right, it continued for a good distance, as far as the flashlight's beam would project before shadows swallowed it up.

"More airflow this way," Shane noted, gesturing to the right. There was only the faintest air movement, but there was a freshness to it. Somewhere down there was an exit, or some ventilation at the very least.

Connor headed right without commentary, his pace revealing his impatience. He was not as careful as Shane would have been in his position, at the head of the pack in an unknown place. He kept Val with him, but if Switchyard were to attack or some trap had been laid, the odds were that Connor would take the brunt of it.

Akerman was sent to the rear of the group, his gun at his side as per

Connor's instructions. Shane didn't like having the jittery mercenary back there and fully armed, but for the time being, he seemed to have calmed down a little.

Another intersection came within a dozen yards. The hallway broke left and right down identical hallways. They continued straight, and an equal distance ahead, they came to another identical junction.

"These must be rooms or something," Connor suggested, touching one of the walls. They had not seen a door anywhere, and Shane was not convinced.

"We don't know how far underground we are. This could just be solid earth."

"Someone built it," Connor pointed out. "You don't just build hallways underground for no reason."

"Didn't say there was no reason," Shane replied. He had little interest in explaining things to Connor. Let the man think what he wanted to think. He was fast becoming contentious now that they seemed to be closing in on their target. Gone was the friendly and helpful Connor who just happened to show up in a pinch and was just trying to make an innocent buck. That veneer had completely faded.

Connor stopped when they reached the third crossroads, looking left, right, and forward.

"There has to be something down here we're missing. We could walk for hours without finding anything."

"You have a plan?" Shane asked.

"Backtrack. Start mapping hallway by hallway, cover every inch, and work our way up and down until no hallway is overlooked."

"Thought you didn't want to waste hours," Shane said.

"It's efficient. It'll save us time in the long run."

Shane was about to reply when Val moved alongside them, taking Shane's wrist in her cold hand.

"Too late," she said.

Akerman screamed. He was only a few feet behind Shane, but he collapsed to his knees, his hands reaching for his head as Shane turned to see Switchyard's pale face, the ghost crouching down on the young man.

The pulpy, bloody mouth stretched, and it took Shane a moment to realize it was a smile. The ghost's fingers were buried in the flesh of Akerman's head. He had slipped them under the skin on either side of his face. With a wet, shucking sound he pulled up, tearing Akerman's scalp from his skull.

Shane moved quickly, running at the ghost. Switchyard kicked Akerman forward, forcing him against Shane and slowing him down. The mercenary screamed as blood poured down his face from the wound, and he clutched at Shane like a drowning man desperate to be saved.

The ghost was gone as quickly as he had appeared. Val vanished in pursuit, fading into the brickwork hallway, leaving Connor and Shane to deal with Akerman's wound.

"You need to calm down, Akerman," Connor said, joining Shane and trying to get the young mercenary to let go of Shane and stop screaming.

"Scalp wounds can bleed a man out," Shane warned him. "They don't always look serious, but they'll kill."

"This doesn't look serious to you?" Connor asked. The ghost had torn away the flesh, leaving only shreds. The blood was significant and already coated the man's face and chest.

Shane opened Akerman's vest and pulled his knife to slice his shirt open from waist to collar. He then pulled the garment from his body and wrapped it as securely as he could around the soldier's head, pulling it tight and creating a small, ragged bandage to staunch the bleeding.

"Am I gonna die?" Akerman cried, shaking his head back and forth. The blood flow had slowed, but it still ran down his face, though most soaked into the shirt. It was a bare-bones bandage at best, but Shane could think of nothing else to help. The man needed a hospital if he had any hope of surviving.

"No. We got the bleeding stopped for now," Connor assured him. "You gotta relax though, Akerman. You hear me? You get worked up, you're going to make it worse. You need to stay calm."

"He ripped my head off. He ripped my goddamn head off," the soldier wailed.

Connor leaned in closer to Akerman's face.

"He cut you up good; I'm not going to lie. But you can make it if you calm the hell down and do what I say. Can you do that? Do you want to stay alive?"

"I want to stay alive!" Tears ran through the blood on his face.

Shane had nothing to add. Connor was lying. Akerman was going to bleed to death. Even if they walked him straight out right then and there, he would never get to a hospital in time. But it was better than letting him panic and die in fear.

If this had been an accident in a factory, an ambulance could have gotten to him in time. Even then, Shane had not seen a scalp wound like that in his life.

"Please don't let me die down here," Akerman begged.

"You got anything for pain?" Shane asked. Connor shook his head.

"Didn't bring kits," he said. Shane's stare was blank, and the other man shrugged. "Took up too much room. Replaced them with lead boxes."

"Solid choice." Shane sighed. He had no reason to care if Akerman lived or died. The man's stupidity had already gotten others killed. But now Connor's ignorance was going to get him killed.

"I'm gonna die. Please don't let me die!"

Shane knew there was nothing they could do. Nonetheless, he stood, picking up Akerman with him.

"Let's go, soldier," he said. "Let's finish what we came for and get you out of here."

"Thank you," Akerman said, more tears coming down his face as he groaned in pain. "I don't want to die down here. I don't want to die."

*We don't always get what we want*, Shane thought. But he said nothing.

# Chapter 22
# Welcome to My Parlor

"He likes pain," Shane said, practically dragging Akerman at this point. The soldier had his arms draped around Connor and Shane's shoulders. They had to carry him at an angle since all three could not walk side by side in the narrow hallway. Carrying him horizontally was not an option because the lower his head went, the faster he'd bleed out.

By Shane's estimate, the soldier had minutes of life left. It didn't make sense to carry him, but he was not about to unburden Connor of his responsibility. He had brought Akerman and the others down there. Everyone else was dead; Connor could literally shoulder this responsibility until it was over.

"What?" Connor asked. He was at the rear of their diagonal walk, with Shane taking the lead. Akerman's head had slumped slightly, and the shirt on his head was saturated with blood. Sometimes, he would awkwardly try to help walking, his feet stumbling and barely responsive before he passed out again.

"Switchyard. He's a sadist. He's playing this like a game."

"I noticed," Connor said.

"All the more reason to destroy him when we can," Shane said. "You want to risk him getting loose when you have him back home or wherever you plan to take him?"

"He won't get loose," Connor countered.

Shane had to laugh.

"You knew West. Did you know Arthur Hempstead? Finley down in Florida? Your supplier in the cemetery? I can guarantee they thought they had a handle on their collections, too."

"How many of them would still be alive if they hadn't met you?"

"You think they died because of me?"

"I do," Connor answered. Shane grinned in the dark, though his companion couldn't see it.

"There's a flaw in using that logic to support capturing Switchyard," Shane said.

"Do tell," Connor replied, mild sarcasm present in his voice.

"You've met me, too."

"Yeah, but we have a deal," the cultist said. It was the second time that had come up. "Unless you're saying you plan to back out on your word."

"Man's only as good as his word," Shane told him. He didn't need to kill Connor to stop Switchyard. Even if he did, breaking his word to a liar would not cause Shane to lose sleep. Connor had played him since they met.

Val had not returned from chasing after Switchyard. There was a chance the ghost had found her, but it wasn't likely. Connor must have had her haunted item on him somewhere, and if she was destroyed, the item would explode, too. She could have just as easily been avoiding them, or even negotiating a deal with the other ghost.

Shane still wasn't sure whether Val would turn on them. In truth, he was more confident that Switchyard wouldn't agree to such a thing rather than Val not giving it a try. Switchyard was not a ghost who worked with others. He was the king of his underground world, that had been made abundantly clear.

Navigating the underground would not keep Akerman alive for very long, Shane knew. He understood Connor's desire for a thorough search, but they needed to do something bolder if they planned to see sunlight again.

Shane was growing tired. They had traveled too long and done too much already. Switchyard was hunting them—toying with them, really—and wasting more time would just give the ghost a greater advantage.

"This way," Shane said, pausing at one of the crossroads of hallways and looking right.

"We need to do a search grid," Connor insisted.

Shane shook his head.

"No. We need to go this way."

"You have psychic powers now, too?"

Shane grunted. This would have been a valuable time to have Thomas Coulson and his skillset handy. But he didn't need psychic powers.

"No. I can smell fresh air."

The faint whiff of air that was not stale had come and gone during their walk, but it was stronger to the right. Had the rest of the place not smelled like a crypt, he might never have noticed. But there was something different down that way, and so far, they had come across nothing different beyond a skeleton nailed to a wall.

Shane pulled at Akerman and forced Connor to come with him, shuffling the barely conscious man onward. The mercenary had stopped making even soft moans and grunts when he stumbled over his feet. In fact, he was no longer moving his feet. Shane and Connor were carrying him.

Shane continued onward, ignoring the dead weight at his shoulder and using his free hand to scan the path ahead with a flashlight. They had gone past another crossroads and seemed to be approaching another when Shane began to worry that he'd misjudged where he was going. Maybe the current of air followed a circuitous path or even came through a crack in the bricks he hadn't noticed. Maybe he'd made a mistake.

The new crossroads approached, and Shane swept the flashlight from right to left. The right path went back to somewhere close to where they had entered, he was sure. But the left caused him to stop.

It was not a pathway like he had expected. Instead, set into the brick, was a door. Not a green door like in the subway stations, but an old, riveted iron door with thin wooden panels set into it and a sign that had mostly faded to rust.

"Maintenance," Shane said, making out enough of the letters to read it. Something had scuffed the floor in front of the door, and the dust caked on it was moist.

"What?" Connor asked. With Akerman's body between them, he didn't have a good view of the door.

"It's a maintenance door," Shane said, his voice low. A noise came from beyond it, something he had only vaguely noticed at first.

"Open it!" Connor insisted.

"Shhh." Shane leaned closer. He could hear something through the metal, a constant, low hum that varied slightly but never ceased. It sounded like static from an old television.

"What?" Connor demanded.

"Just shut up for a minute," Shane replied. "I can hear something."

Shane waited, ear nearly touching the door, getting a sense of what it was. It was not the ghost. It was too constant, machine-like. There was a familiarity to it that he could not place. Not a boiler working in the basement, and certainly not an engine, but something.

"Shane," Connor said.

He blocked the man out. If they opened the door without knowing what they were getting into, they could all be dead in a flash.

"Shane!"

"What?" he growled, looking back. Suddenly Akerman's weight increased, and he nearly slipped from Shane's shoulder. He realized then that Connor had dropped the man.

Unprepared to shoulder Akerman alone, he struggled for a moment and then shifted his weight, easing the mercenary to the floor.

"What are you doing?" Shane asked. He didn't need the other man to answer. He could feel it as he eased Akerman to a seated position.

The mercenary's body flopped to the left. Shane had to pull him upright and balance him, his legs splayed out before him. Even still, his head lolled to one side.

Shane touched his neck, holding the tips of his fingers to Akerman's carotid artery. He counted silently. Not the heartbeats, but the five seconds that passed during which he felt nothing at all. Akerman was dead.

"No sense carrying a corpse around," Connor said. He was right, but Shane still stood and punched him in the nose once more.

"Jesus!" Connor growled through gritted teeth. Shane had already damaged it badly before. "What the hell is wrong with you?"

"Nothing," he replied.

He looked down at Akerman again. The mercenary was an idiot. Too young and too poorly trained to be doing what he did. That was his fault. But it was also Connor's fault for bringing him to a job he couldn't handle. It was a poor way to run an operation. Connor deserved more than a broken nose for that.

"You lay a hand on me again and our deal is off," Connor said, his voice steady and cold. It was the first time he sounded like someone from the Endless Night and not the person he claimed to be.

"There's my bloodthirsty cultist," Shane said. "Get yourself ready. There's something behind the door."

Connor shifted gears quickly, ignoring his nose and Shane in favor of their new target.

"What is it?"

It was an obvious question, but one to which Shane had no answer. If he had a thousand chances to plan the mission they were on, he would have picked a thousand better ways to go about doing what they were about to do. But at that moment, he couldn't think of anything more appropriate.

"Let's find out," he said, taking the door by the handle and pushing it open into the darkness beyond.

## Chapter 23
## End of the Line

The door opened more easily than such an ancient thing had a right to. Shane pushed it in with little warning, giving Connor no time to prepare for what could have waited beyond.

The noise could have been a trap waiting to kill them. It could have been another ghost, grinding away at some ungodly weapon. It could have been the steady roar of an ancient machine for all Shane knew. But it was none of those things.

Connor cursed as he tried to see into the darkened room. Shane was now convinced he was not who he pretended to be. His story about stumbling into a new position in the cult after West and the others vacated was too convenient. The idea that he only wanted to collect ghosts for money was not believable, either. The man was good at playing his character, but not that good. He let too many little things slip. And the threat in the hallway was the last straw for Shane.

Whether the entire Cult of the Endless Night had been dissolved and reformed with Connor or whether he was one of West's underlings rising in his wake, the result was the same. He was going to use the ghosts he captured to get what he wanted. Money, power, whatever he desired. And he would kill to do so.

Connor's disregard for the life of his team showed the kind of man he was. And the indifference to Akerman in his dying moments was enough to convince Shane that the deal they had made was no deal at all. Connor would kill him as soon as he had possession of Switchyard. The only reason he had left Shane alive this long was to use him. Shane was a weapon Connor needed. If he couldn't control Shane after Switchyard and use him for more targets, Connor would turn on him. More likely, he'd send someone else to do it. Maybe even Val.

Shane could have killed him then and there, but he still needed to find Martin. And as much as Connor was using him, he also needed Connor. Switchyard had just as much reason to want Connor dead as he did Shane. The cultist could prove a reasonable distraction in the final minutes while Shane figured out how to save Martin and eliminate Switchyard. Time would tell.

Standing in the doorway, a blast of humid but fresh air hit the duo. The sound of water rushing in the distance filled the room and echoed back on itself. The chamber was like a living, breathing thing. Its hot, damp breath rushed from the darkness and covered the men as they entered.

"Water," Connor said. "It sounds like a river."

He was right, but Shane knew they couldn't be near the river. And even if they had traveled that far, it couldn't be where Switchyard was based. The distance was too far.

Whatever they had stumbled upon was something Shane had never heard of. It was probably something no one had heard of in decades, if not longer.

Shane swept the room with the beam of the flashlight. It looked like something from an antique warship. The walls were lined with pipes, some fixed with small shut-off valves and others with ones as large as dinner plates.

Most of the pipes looked rusted, but some were newer than others, relative though that term was. It was the difference between hundred-year-old plumbing and hundred-and-fifty-year-old plumbing. Pipes rose into the ceiling and vanished to parts unknown while water dripped profusely from several.

"What the hell is this?" Connor asked. Shane shook his head. He couldn't imagine what was hooked to such ancient pipes below the city that might still be in use. Maybe it was like the first station he had found, where someone had never shut off the water even after years of disuse.

There was no way anyone was still making use of the room. The hallways had no sign of human footprints in ages. And even if someone had come down to do maintenance, surely Switchyard would have made short work of them.

"Doesn't matter," Shane pointed out. It could have been Capone's lost vault for all the difference it made. It was the likeliest place to find Martin they had come across since leaving the camp by Tremont.

Shane scanned from one side of the room to the other, halting the flashlight's beam on the right wall. A door had been broken in, long ago from the look of the rust, and with extreme force. The metal had buckled as though broken with a battering ram, the dents and bends orange with rust.

The hall beyond was the source of the rushing water sound, and it echoed up the path loud and clear. The current of the air was not fast, but it was constant. Something was moving steadily, and it was not far off.

Shane moved to lead the way when a face emerged from the hall, peering around the corner in the light of his flashlight. Red lips parted in a smile.

"What took you so long?" Val asked. She crept from the hallway into the maintenance room, her silver hair partially obscuring her eyes.

"Where were you?" Connor demanded. The ghost gestured noncommittally to the surrounding room.

"Here, obviously. I followed Switchyard here. It's his home."

"Did you find his item?"

"Didn't get close enough," Val admitted. "He's strong."

"You're dead," Connor pointed out. The ghost glanced at Shane.

"Can still get deader."

"Is he in here for sure?" Connor asked, shifting gears. Val nodded.

"Down the hall. He made a… lair? Shrine? Not sure what to call it."

"Sounds promising," Shane said. Val smiled awkwardly.

"It's not nice."

He wondered what that might have meant coming from a ghost, but he had some ideas. They had seen what Switchyard was capable of. The place he called home, the place where he had most probably taken Martin, would be a dark place in more ways than one.

"Have you seen Martin?" Shane asked.

"There is a man," Val confirmed. "Unconscious but alive. And restrained."

"Restrained?" Connor asked. The ghost nodded.

"Rope, maybe? I couldn't see, but he is bound."

Connor looked at Shane. Martin was a worm on a hook, then. Bait in the trap to get them to bite.

Shane didn't think they were going to surprise Switchyard, but he had hoped there was a chance to at least overwhelm him. Their advantage was now slim, and the ghost would have prepared for that. Hell, he'd had more than a century to perfect his lair and arrange for what to do if intruders arrived.

"What do you think?" Connor asked. The way he switched from antagonistic to collaborative as the situation demanded was almost admirable. Shane figured he was the kind of man who would have managed to get a lifeboat on the Titanic all to himself.

"I think this is a trap," Shane answered. Connor shrugged.

"Obviously. What do we do?"

"Funny how it's 'we' when you need someone to stand in front of a threat."

"I'm being practical," Connor told him. "You can destroy ghosts and I can't. We both want Switchyard; you just happen to want Martin as well. We'll have to work together, or we'll both die."

"I could just get Martin and leave," Shane pointed out. Connor smiled and shook his head.

"No, you can't. Your fight with Switchyard is personal now. Plus, you hate me enough to want to ruin my plans."

"That worked well for you, huh?" Shane said.

"It did," Connor agreed.

Shane had underestimated Connor. Not that he had ever fully believed him, but he had certainly rigged the game in his favor. As much as it could be rigged. There was still every reason to believe they were both about to die.

"How long can you keep Switchyard busy?" Connor asked Val. The ghost's expression became pensive, and she shook her head.

"I don't think I can do that," she answered. Connor scoffed.

"What's that supposed to mean?"

"Means I'm not here to kill him. Not my niche."

"I just need you to keep him on the ropes while we find his item and get him boxed up. You're not supposed to kill him," Connor explained.

"He might destroy me, is what I'm saying," she clarified. "He's been doing this a long time. He's good at hunting. And we're in his territory."

"So, you're saying you *won't* do it? Not that you can't."

Connor's voice had become emotionless once more. His body language stiffened, and his demeanor was off. If Shane had to guess, he was in the process of changing plans in his head.

"I'm saying I can't do it. Maybe if Shane and I fight him together…"

She looked at Shane, a hopeful smile on her face. She spoke as though she were proposing a date.

"I don't think Connor wants me putting my hand in his Cracker Jack box to snatch his prize. But if you can help me free Martin, I'll help you with Switchyard."

Val's smile widened, and Connor sighed.

"I'm so glad I got to play matchmaker for you two," he said. "Let's go."

Connor went into the hallway. They had no plan to speak of, but Connor's patience was wearing thin. Shane followed him with Val, heading toward the sound of rushing water.

The distance was short, thirty feet at most, and the hallway branched left. Connor had only just turned the corner when he stopped again. The hallway ended abruptly, opening to a much larger room.

It must have been used as equipment storage in the past, though there was no way to tell. It was large, nearly gymnasium-sized, with more thick pipes running along the ceiling.

The floor of the room was torn up, the rock roughly excavated with no apparent rhyme or reason. It looked like massive rats had chewed apart the stone, with some spots missing chunks of stone no bigger than cinder blocks and other spots gutted deeply enough to make pits that could hide a man.

The largest excavation was in the center of the room, a deep pit that had been dug down until it exposed the source of the noise that was now so loud Shane could hear nothing else. An underground river rushed beneath the floor, the white, frothy water churning around the hole that exposed it. The rushing water was about ten feet down, and there was only a small patch of stone on either side. If they fell into the pit, it would not be easy to get out without being swept away.

Whether Switchyard had dug the hole himself or someone else had exposed the river, Shane couldn't guess. The hole the mystery digger had created was big enough to swallow a small automobile. Shane wondered if whoever had built the place for the city of Boston had discovered and then abandoned it because it rendered the entire subterranean facility unsafe. Would they have left a rushing river exposed to anyone who came across it? He was unsure what kind of standards were in place a century ago.

Connor let his flashlight sweep across the rest of the room. No one spoke, not even Val, as the light exposed what Switchyard had done to the long-forgotten room.

Bones lined the walls to the right and left. Bones of every kind, from the smallest finger and toe joints to ribs and femurs, humeri, and pelvic bones.

Toward the rear of the room, among the pits and plateaus where the most stone had been dug out, there were more elaborate creations. Things that looked like totem poles assembled from corpses. A few were still fresh enough to have meat on them, while others had long ago rotted to skeletal remains.

Skins hung from the walls, some spread into nearly perfect human shapes, others wrinkled and formless scraps. Shane's eyes fell on one in particular. It was a face. Switchyard had removed someone's face and pinned it to the wall.

The arrangement of the corpse and skeleton shrines seemed deliberate and balanced. Where one was placed to the left, it was mirrored to the right. The culmination of years of work. Years of murder.

Connor fixed the light on the center of the room, past the exposed river, to the far wall. Martin was slumped on the ground, his hands bound behind him as Val had said. He lay in a pile of filth, the remains of an indeterminate number of bodies.

"Where is he?" Connor whispered. Val shook her head.

"Can't see him," she said.

*He's hiding*, Shane thought. *Watching and waiting to strike.*

"You two head around that side," Shane said, pointing to the left. "I'd go to the right." The exposed river was in a chasm in the center of the room, but there was space to walk around it on the sides. Switchyard would only be able to go for one or the other if they split around it.

Connor would be looking for Switchyard's haunted item, Shane knew. But the room was dark and cluttered, and whatever they were searching for would not be easy to find. They didn't even know what it was. It would be dumb luck at best to find it.

"Be fast," Shane warned. Switchyard was watching. Martin was the bait. They only had moments before they tripped the trap.

And he planned on doing exactly what the ghost wanted.

## Chapter 24
# Switchyard

Shane didn't wait to see what Connor and Val were doing. He didn't need Connor anymore because he couldn't trust him. There, in Switchyard's lair, the man's only goal would be to find and capture the ghost. Shane had no time for that.

He darted right around the river chasm, kicking aside stray bones and old bits of clothing left over from the ghost's victims. The smell of the river mixed with the smell of old, damp, rotted flesh.

Shane had to get to Martin quickly. He closed the gap between them, keeping his light fixed on Martin's unmoving body. On the far side of the chasm, he could see Val and Connor moving as well, but at a slower pace. Connor was searching for the item, whatever it might be. Shane needed to be faster, he just didn't know if it was possible.

Something moved behind Martin and Shane stopped, keeping his light fixed. Seconds passed, and he started moving again slowly, not wanting to waste time but not wanting to be too reckless either. He had already pushed his luck too many times with Switchyard.

More movement caught his eye. Switchyard's pale, purple-veined hand crept up and over Martin's body. It wrapped around him from the side, palm down against Martin's chest he was hugging the man.

Then Switchyard's face appeared, peering over the top of Martin's shoulder, his eyes fixed on Shane. The ghost's pulpy, gnarled mouth twisted into something akin to a smile. Nearly black blood spilled over his lips and ran down his chin. He said nothing but let his hand drift up along Martin's chest to his throat.

Shane was too far away. If he had broken into a run, Switchyard would still have had plenty of time to snap Martin's neck or something worse.

Shane's eyes darted left and right. Connor could see what was happening as well and had slowed his pace, but Val continued forward, creeping around the chasm, bent over like an animal stalking its prey.

Her attention was focused on Switchyard. Her silver hair fell to cover her face almost completely. Her hands bent and twisted like claws, gripping rock as she crawled slowly and cautiously toward the other spirit.

"Val," Connor yelled. Switchyard's attention left Shane. The ghost concentrated on Val now, his thick, dagger-like nails pushing into Martin's throat. "We are not here to fight him."

Shane cursed silently. Val was willing to distract the ghost, even fight him despite saying she would not, and Connor was trying to call her off. He knew Martin's life was on the line, he just didn't care. Shane guessed he was hoping for it. Martin was the distraction he needed. If he could find Switchyard's haunted item, he could take it in the chaos and make a run for it. He'd still need a backup plan to stop Shane, of course. But what mattered most was Switchyard's item.

If Connor couldn't get Switchyard to take Shane out, then he needed a Plan B to save himself and ensure he got away with the ghost without Shane stopping him. There were only so many ways that would work. He was still armed with the iron slug bullets and a sidearm. They didn't do much to ghosts, but they would kill Shane.

Val looked at Shane and parted her hair just enough so he could see her smile. She was not creating a distraction for Connor; she was creating one for Shane. They could rush the ghost together. They could back him into a corner and maybe save Martin while the ghost looked to save himself. Switchyard had already proved smart enough to want to avoid direct confrontation. He preferred an opportunistic style of combat.

"Val, I'm warning you," Connor shouted. He shifted the flashlight beam while Val's glow kept Switchyard illuminated enough to keep an eye on him.

Connor stood with his arm out over the chasm, his fist closed tight.

"Don't," Val said, her voice close to a hiss. Shane couldn't see what Connor held.

"You had your orders," Connor said.

"It's a distraction," the ghost insisted. Connor shook his head. He glanced at Shane.

"It's a betrayal," he told her. "And I don't need the uncertainty."

He opened his hand. Val screamed in rage, and something small and metallic glinted. It fell into the river and was rushed away. Shane had no idea what it was, but Val's reaction was unmistakable. Connor had just dropped her haunted item into the river.

The silver-haired ghost ran at him, a bestial shriek rising. The river moved at a fast pace and Shane had no idea where it headed or how far it traveled. But if it swept her far enough away, it would pull her from the room entirely.

Val rushed at Connor, who stood his ground and raised his gun, pulling the trigger at point-blank range. The iron slug passed through her body and she vanished, forced back to the object now carried away from the room at breakneck speed.

Shane stared at him, the chasm between them, and Connor smiled back. There was nothing Shane could do or say. So he said nothing, and the other man shrugged.

"Don't look so upset," he shouted over the sound of the water, pulling his flashlight out. He directed it to the far side of the room, where Switchyard still hid behind Martin.

"Be a buddy and show me what I'm looking for," Connor asked. He pointed the beam of light directly at the ghost's face and then, without pause, pulled the trigger a second time.

The muzzle flare was a quick burst of orange and then Switchyard was gone.

*Huh, smarter than you look*, Shane thought. He made his break for Martin in Switchyard's absence and Connor did the same. They both finished circling the chasm but where Shane made a move for the unconscious man, Connor swept the room with his light until he caught sight of the pale spirit rising from a spot near the back wall, the smallest of the bone shrines, where a skull sat alone among some stone debris.

The skull was old and yellowed with age. The jaw was broken, and many of the teeth were missing. The pattern of missing teeth was one Shane instantly recognized as the same mess inside Switchyard's broken and swollen jaw. It was his skull, the centerpiece of the shrine he had made.

Connor had shot Switchyard to force the ghost's hand. The iron slug made him return, if just for a moment, to his haunted item, revealing what it was. Connor had his target, he just had to get to it while Shane got to Martin. Switchyard would have to choose who to attack. Their fate was in the hands of a psychotic ghost flipping a coin.

Shane moved for Martin. The ghost, several yards beyond, opened his mouth and howled. The sound was not something that should have come from a person, or anything that had ever been alive. It was the sound of fear and hate and anger.

But switchyard did not attack. Rather than choose which of the men to head for, the ghost raised his hands and spread his arms wide. Shane made it to Martin's side and hit the ground, kneeling in a pool of congealed blood as he reached for the man's wrists. They were bound with thin wire. He began pulling at it while Connor circled Switchyard, cautious of where he was in relation to his skull that was only a foot or two behind the ghost.

"Ryan!"

Connor's voice carried over the rush of the river and through the unearthly cry from the ghost. Shane lifted his head, watching in the light from Connor's flashlight. The ghost's arms were still, but the flesh was moving. It pulsed like a thing alive, and the thick, purple veins beneath the surface wriggled and squirmed like thick worms. They had pierced through the ghost's flesh and were freeing themselves, writhing upward toward the ceiling, fat and glistening.

Veins and arteries and capillaries protruded from the ghost's flesh and rose into the air. Soon, they were as long as the ghost's arms, and then longer still. Not worms but serpents. Living ropes, thick and gelatinous and moving as though they had minds of their own.

Some of the veins branched forward, weaving through the air toward Connor and Shane. Most went up, until they wound around the pipes on the ceiling.

The veins lifted Switchyard's body like a marionette. They grew longer still, extending further and further, reaching across the lengths of pipe, and creating a network of pulsing, squirming veins like a spider web.

Connor watched in awe. Shane returned to his work, not interested in the ghost's theatrics. He had no time. Martin had no time.

He pulled the wire away roughly and shook Martin as he lifted him to a seated position. He was still alive, Shane could see his chest rising and falling, but the blood down the side of his face was only partially from the filth Switchyard had dropped him in. Shane needed him awake if there was any hope of getting out alive.

Shane shook him again and gave him a light slap across the face. Maybe not the best cure for head trauma, but he needed something.

"Martin, we need to get moving," Shane urged, shaking him again. He groaned and Shane reached into the chasm, collecting a handful of water from the river, then slapped him again.

Martin's eyes fluttered, looked about aimlessly, and then fixed on Shane for a moment before he started choking.

A thick, purple tube slipped around Martin's throat and squeezed tightly as it throbbed and continued to encircle his neck a second time. Martin's eyes went wide, but he was unable to even gasp as the vein crushed his windpipe.

Shane grabbed the serpentine appendage and pulled. It felt like cold slime in his hands, resisting him and collapsing in his grip. He squeezed as tightly as he could, pulling slack away from Switchyard to loop around one fist before twisting.

The phantom vein snapped like an elastic band. The segment around Martin's neck vanished while the part still attached to Switchyard slithered back to the ghost's body.

Martin choked and nearly doubled over before Shane caught him.

"We have to get out of here now."

"Shane?" Martin croaked, blinking and shaking his head. Shane yanked him to his feet as another vein snaked around his ankle.

"Move or die."

Shane's legs came out from under him. The veins worked like tentacles, plucking him and raising him into the air. More had already taken hold of Connor, and he wrestled helplessly in their grasp, unable to fight back as Shane had. Martin stumbled toward the exit on unsteady feet. He made it only several steps before Switchyard snared him once again, pulling him back.

Shane cursed, wrestling with the wriggling arms that came for him, seeking to choke him or snake down his throat. He bit through one and tore a second into pieces as more began pulling on his arms and legs.

"Shoot him," Shane yelled, trying to get Connor's attention. A new vein slithered into his mouth, cold as ice and quivering like jelly. He felt it surge past his tongue to the back of his throat. He gagged and bit hard, his teeth crushing the thick, unliving tissue until it ceased to exist.

One of the tendrils managed to ensnare Shane's left wrist and held tightly enough that he could no longer bring his hands together. It pulled hard toward the ceiling as another on his ankle pulled down.

Pain shot up Shane's body as he was forced in opposite

directions. His skin felt like it would tear, and his bones threatened to pop out of joints. There was nothing left for him to grab, nothing to fight with as the veins and arteries pulled at his appendages.

A new tentacle wrapped around his neck, circling once and then twice as it began to squeeze. The pressure built slowly and his vision blurred. He struggled some more, but the veins trapped his arms and legs in an iron grip.

Shane clenched his teeth and held in a scream of pain. The sound of a gunshot overwhelmed all other noise for the briefest of moments, and then he was falling.

It lasted only a heartbeat. He was in the air and then there was nothing. Switchyard vanished, and Shane hit the stone floor with a grunt.

Connor must have gotten a shot off, must have hit the ghost, and sent it back to the skull once more. But Shane had no time to consider what had happened.

Martin's scream joined the sound of rushing water. Shane rolled over in time to see the man thrown into the chasm above the river. He got to his hands and knees, grabbing the flashlight where it had fallen.

Connor's bullet had rendered Switchyard useless, if only for a moment. It had also passed unobstructed through the ghost's body into the pipes on the ceiling. Shane couldn't tell if it had hit more than one pipe or if one blew and took others, but a massive stream of pressurized water had erupted into the room and was quickly flooding everything.

The level of water above the river chasm had already begun to rise. The room was flooding, and they'd all be swept away with the current, probably down through the river just as Val had been.

The only difference was that she was already dead. The others would be dead soon.

# Chapter 25
# To the Victor Go the Spoils

Shane scrambled around the chasm to the far side above Martin. The spray from the overhead pipes saturated the room from wall to wall and he could see almost nothing else. Bones and bodies washed away in the flow, filling the chasm and getting sucked away by the river.

Connor had vanished, and Switchyard had not returned. There was no sound beyond the roar of water above and below. It was deafening and all-consuming.

Shane reached the far edge of the chasm and shouted for Martin. He might as well have been calling for someone on the far side of the world. He couldn't even hear himself.

Shane pointed the flashlight down, flicking the light on and off. Martin looked up, shielding his face from the burst pipes. Though he had been pushed to the far side of the pit, the water level had risen enough that he was essentially in the river now, with his feet and ankles underwater as the levels continued to rise.

Martin shouted something, but his words were lost in the chaos. It was enough that he could see Shane and knew he was there. They just needed to get out.

Shane slipped from the backpack he had put on when he fought Switchyard's guard dogs. It still held the four captured spirits in lead-lined boxes.

Shane dumped the contents into the river. The boxes were immediately swept away, sucked into the water. He lowered the straps on one side of the pack for Martin after wrapping the others tightly around his hand. Martin grabbed hold and began to climb as Shane pulled. The roar of water continued unabated. Switchyard had not returned, and Connor had not surfaced, either.

Shane groaned, gritting his teeth from the strain, and pulled with all his strength. Martin kicked and scuttled up the wall until his hands gripped the sides of the chasm. Together, they maneuvered him onto the stone, where he collapsed in another fit of coughing.

"Move," Shane shouted, the words vanishing in the deluge as he pulled the other man up by his collar. Even without hearing, Martin understood. He got to his feet and stumbled toward the exit.

From the doorway, Shane directed the light back into the room. Water, white and furious, created a wall that nearly blocked the far side of the space. Most of Switchyard's trophies were gone.

He pushed Martin forward, and they ran back to the maintenance room and out into the hallway. There were no footprints save for the ones they had left on their way in. Akerman's corpse still lay slumped against the wall. No one had escaped. Connor was still there somewhere.

"Where are we?" Martin asked, still gasping for air. Shane shook his head.

"No idea. Let's go."

He led Martin in the opposite direction he had taken on the way in. He had not seen Switchyard, and that meant the ghost could show up anywhere at any time. They needed a fast escape. The problem was he didn't know if such a thing existed.

They ran down the hall. Shane had created a map in his head, not just of the basement hallways but of the underground he had traveled to get that far. He was almost positive that they faced subway tunnels and were headed east. If they were under Boston Common, they would be heading east, back to the start of Tremont. Back to where Jaker had first taken him underground. At least, that was Shane's best guess.

"We have to slow down," Martin wheezed. Shane turned the light on him, stopping for a moment.

"I came down here with a half-dozen guys. It's just us now. We're not stopping."

He tugged on Martin's shirt and forced him to keep running. They ignored several branches in the halls and kept going straight until they found an end to the tunnel in the form of a brick wall.

Left or right were the only choices. Right led back in the general direction of where Shane had entered, back to the chambers where Switchyard had left his guards. But those were natural caverns, not constructed ones. The wall was destroyed to allow access to the maze Shane was in now. Which meant the real exit was somewhere else.

He broke left, still forcing Martin with him. The rush of water echoed through the basement, sometimes sounding near and sometimes distant. Shane wondered what the source of the water was. The pipes were massive, and for a city like Boston, there could have been a nearly endless supply coming down those lines from somewhere. It was going to ruin someone's day when they realized what had happened and how they'd need to repair it, but that was not his problem. His only concern was making sure they escaped before the hallways flooded.

"What happened to Connor?" Martin shouted.

"No idea," Shane answered.

"We have to... we can't just leave him."

"We can and we are," Shane replied. "He's not who you thought he was."

"The hell does that mean?"

Shane slowed down, scanning the hallway ahead with the flashlight.

"You know the guys who have been coming down here, using people as bait for Switchyard?"

Martin nodded, holding the wound on the side of his head, and breathing heavily.

"That's Connor. His people. His group."

"What? There's no way."

"They're called the Endless Night. They capture ghosts. Sell them. Use them to kill. Whatever they need."

Martin scoffed, shaking his head.

"He's homeless. That doesn't even make sense."

"He was playing you. He convinced you to call me because he knew I could get him to Switchyard."

"How would he even know I knew you?" Martin asked.

"You told him. Not that it matters. They know about me. They know about Canada and the people I met there. Your cousin and you."

"He planned all this?"

Martin's face said he still didn't believe it. But Shane didn't care that much. While it did seem like Connor was trapped or even dead, Shane's greater concern was that Switchyard had not appeared. There was no reason for the ghost to be missing for so long. The water would have meant nothing to him. Even if the skull had been lost, he would have had time to fight back before he was swept too far away. Shane assumed that meant he couldn't reappear because Connor had captured him.

They started moving again, following the wall to the end of the hallway until they found another metal door.

"Someone was just here," Martin observed. They stared at the door, left open by whoever had passed through it last. Shane directed the flashlight beam to the floor. Footsteps in the dust led from the door down to parts unknown. There were splatters in the dust as well; small and barely noticeable. Water droplets that had accumulated into tiny balls of mud. He bent down and touched one. Still cold and wet.

He directed the beam into the room beyond the door. Another tiny room, only this one housed a set of metal stairs that led upward.

There must have been a door Shane hadn't seen in the dark, on one of the back walls beyond Switchyard. Connor had escaped.

"Come on," he said, leading Martin to the stairs. He wanted to get back into some fresh air and a dry set of clothes.

※

The stairs led Shane and Martin up to the basement of the Park Street Church, across the street from Boston Common. They were a stone's throw from the station where he'd first gone underground with Jaker.

It was late and the sky was dark when they made their way outside. The streets were still alive with traffic and the sounds of city life. There was no sign of Connor anywhere, nor did Shane expect there to be.

"You think he got the ghost?" Martin asked once they were outside.

"Probably," Shane said.

"So what now?"

"Now you leave town. Go back home. Go to Jamaica, I don't care. Get away from this place for a while."

"Yeah," Martin agreed. "That's probably a good idea. I just… I don't think I can go home. It's still—"

"Like I said," Shane interrupted. "Anywhere but here."

Martin still had problems, ones beyond Shane's ability to fix. But he was alive, and that had to count for something.

They walked a short way together, alongside the park, until Martin caught sight of a bus that would take him to a nearby walk-in clinic. Shane advised him to get his head looked at before he went anywhere. They parted with a simple handshake and nothing else.

Shane looked into the park once he was alone, catching sight of a few ghosts and a few pedestrians. Jaker was probably in there somewhere. He wondered if he was waiting to hear about Shane's success. He shrugged and kept walking. He hadn't really succeeded.

Connor had fled, probably with his prize in hand. The Endless Night was still operating in Boston, and probably beyond, throughout all of Randall West's old territory. But was Connor the man in charge, or just another cog in the machine?

Shane didn't want to know. He wanted to wash his hands off of the whole thing and leave, forget about the Endless Night and their ghosts. But they were not giving him the option.

That meant it was his turn to start hunting.

# Epilogue

"What the hell are you eating?"

"A sandwich. You want some?"

"How can you eat in here?"

The man in the white coat shrugged. Something about the smell of formaldehyde had always made him hungry. He understood the apprehension other people felt when they first discovered it. When you're in a room full of corpses and dismembered body parts and organs, you don't typically think of lunch. But after a month, it was unavoidable. You always thought of lunch. He did, anyway.

He took a bite from the sandwich, a footlong chicken bacon ranch sub with extra pickles and mayo. The pickle crunched, and he chewed, staring down at the table in front of him.

"You're a sick dude, Tate," Bothwell said. He didn't know Bothwell's first name and didn't care much, either. Bothwell worked for the boss, so Curtis Tate did what Bothwell asked. Within reason.

"What am I looking for today, anyway? I didn't get the paperwork," Tate said. They had a shipment that morning and it was bigger than usual.

Things were expanding, he'd been told. It would be fast, and it might be a little overwhelming at first. But they promised him an ungodly amount of money, and that was good enough for him. He'd sit up to his hips in skulls and femurs all day if he had to.

"Kind of a potluck, I guess," Bothwell answered.

"What does that mean?"

"It means it's all uninspected. We don't have anything on any of it yet. Just see what you can find."

Tate sighed.

"Why do you guys send me organs, then? What am I going to do with a liver right now? Is there such a thing as a haunted liver?"

The men stared at each other. Curtis Tate had never been a physically intimidating man. He had planned to become a doctor but had never finished med school. The work he did now wasn't licensed by any board, he just knew enough anatomy and biology to get it done properly. His hand was steady enough with a scalpel. And he was making more selling non-transplant tissue and organs than even the best surgeons would make in ten years.

Bothwell, on the other hand, looked like a highly priced thug. He wore expensive suits that were tailored to his massive frame. Tate guessed he was about six-foot-five and probably close to three hundred pounds. Mostly muscle, but he did have some extra weight on him. His life in a suit was making him soft, Tate guessed. He'd never say that out loud.

The big man kept his hair shaved close, and he carried himself like the other military men Tate had known. He never asked Bothwell about his past, partially because it wasn't his business and partially because he didn't care. He was mostly a courier and a messenger, though they met twice a week to do the work. They weren't friends, they were associates.

"I never heard of haunted anything until three months ago, so what the hell do I know?" Bothwell replied. It was a fair enough answer.

"I keep telling the warehouse guys and the drivers and you and whoever else wants to make this work more efficiently that no one haunts meat. This liver is going to rot, and bugs will eat it, and it'll stink in no time. No ghost is going to hitch its wagon to a liver. It doesn't even make sense. There's an attachment, some kind of investment or importance there. Who the hell cared about their liver so much in life that it snagged their soul in death?"

Bothwell stared at him blankly and shrugged.

"And who cares about their skeleton so much that they haunt it? I don't know, man."

"The skull and the skeleton, those make the frame of the body. That makes sense. It lasts when the living part is stripped away, get it?" Tate explained. "Devoid of a sentimental object at the time of death, a spirit that engages with the living world will root itself to the skeleton at the moment of death, and thus, you have a haunted skeleton."

"Don't act like you know what you're talking about," Bothwell said, laughing.

Tate ignored him, taking another bite of his sandwich. He didn't technically know what he was talking about. It was speculation.

Curtis Tate had begun seeing ghosts after a near-fatal car crash in his early twenties. He'd been clinically dead for about five minutes, and doctors had removed a sliver of metal, a piece of the other car's hood, from his brain.

For nearly two years afterward, he thought brain damage was causing the hallucinations. It wasn't until he'd chanced upon a man who could see the same things that he realized it was real.

His life had mostly fallen into shambles at that point. He'd left medical school, lost his home, and lost his family and friends who couldn't or wouldn't support him. But the Endless Night had been there to pick up the pieces for him. All he had to do was help with a bit of harvesting. Procure ghosts, pack them up, and ship them off.

He felt like an oyster farmer hunting pearl. The group had set up the lab for him, taking donations of human bodies for "science". The government tightly regulated the world of organ donation. But non-transplant tissue was barely monitored. If you offered someone a thousand dollars for the body of a loved one and claimed it was for science, all you needed was a signature to make it legal.

For the people who were reluctant to give their loved one's whole body, they offered discounted cremation plans in exchange for a "partial" donation. That usually meant cremating a hand, giving it to the family, and keeping the rest. Still all legal, still barely regulated. When people saw the cost of funeral expenses, many were happy to get on board. It gave them a sense that their loved one would help people through science and medicine, while also saving them money. Everyone wins.

The company furnished hospitals, medical labs, schools, and anyone else doing tissue research with the parts they didn't need. All you had to do was send one thing off for research to legally fulfill the bargain. You could get an entire human body, send the spleen to a research hospital, and keep the rest for anything. They spent thousands but made millions.

The main goal, of course, was not organ harvesting or selling at all. It was ghosts. Tate had yet to work out a reliable ratio because of the inconsistency in how many living people became ghosts and how many who became ghosts were rooted to an object rather than their body, but there was a significant number of dead bodies that haunted their bones. He managed to harvest two or three per week.

"Do you know how many people die every day in America?" Tate asked, chewing a mouthful of mayo-saturated chicken.

"Not a clue," Bothwell answered.

"Nearly eight thousand. Every day. We only get a fraction donated, but with the increased payout, we're getting more. People who want help with funeral costs, or who think they're being altruistic. We could harvest more than a hundred ghosts a year. Two hundred even, if the pace keeps up."

"Cool," Bothwell said sarcastically. Tate rolled his eyes.

"I don't know what you're getting paid, but that's a lot of money for me, sport."

"So what are you complaining about?"

"This," he answered, shaking a bin of organs. The organs were supposed to be going to the legit facilities that bought them. The lab where he worked only had so much cooler space on hand, so he couldn't fit all the bodies he was sorting along with an abundance of loose tissue. It was inefficient.

"Talk to the tech guys. It's not my job."

"I'm talking to you because you can talk to the boss. I get things are crazy lately, but we're shooting ourselves in the foot here. This slows the process, which slows the money. I should only be getting corpses. Full bodies."

"You can talk to the boss," the big man replied. "Send him a text."

Tate sighed again and set his sandwich on an aluminum table.

"Yeah, that's been working so well. Do you just want to pick up the new guy and go? Let me sort through this mess and see what I can find. Takes a while to strip tissue off bone, anyway."

He had no idea if any of the new bodies were haunted and having Bothwell over his shoulder the whole time would only slow him down further. Best to just get the big man out of his hair and back to the boss. Maybe the thug would forward some of his concerns and get things working more smoothly, but he doubted it.

He led Bothwell out of the lab and down the hall under the buzzing fluorescent bulbs towards the holding cells. He'd never had more than two on hand at a time, but there were six cells just in case. Today, only one was occupied.

Tate punched a security code into a digital pad and entered the room. Three cells on each wall featured what looked like plain glass doors, with a control panel and nothing else.

Inside each cell was a pedestal and a small wooden box. The boxes were lined with lead, and they controlled the mechanism that opened and closed the boxes from outside. All but one of the boxes was open.

Tate began punching in the entry code when Bothwell stopped him.

"Let me see him first," he said.

"What?"

"C'mon," the bigger man said with a grin. "I never get to see them."

Tate's instinct was to say no, for no reason other than Bothwell got on his nerves. But he couldn't help himself. He understood the thrill. Seeing a ghost, especially up close, had been terrifying when he didn't know what was happening, but it was also exhilarating. Now that he understood it, understood who and what they were, it was even more remarkable.

He pressed a green button on the control panel. The gears in the pedestal moved and the lid of the wooden box opened. For a moment nothing happened and then, in a blink of an eye, a man stood between the pedestal and the glass door.

"My God..." Bothwell said quietly. The ghost was once a man in his thirties. He had been murdered, Tate learned, in a botched robbery. Someone had shot him point-blank in the chest with a shotgun. Now, standing in the room, Tate could see clearly through the man's chest to the other side. The hole was about the size of a basketball.

"What the hell is going on?" the ghost demanded. He pounded a hand on the glass, tempered to keep spirits imprisoned. The man had only been a ghost for a few days and during most of that time, Tate had kept him enclosed in the lead box, trapped in his own haunted skull. He probably still had no idea what happened to him.

"Can he feel it?" Bothwell asked, indicating the hole in the man's chest. Tate shook his head.

"As far as I know, they don't feel anything. They can talk and do things, but there's no sensation. They don't sleep or eat or anything."

"Why are some of them psychos?"

Tate laughed. He wasn't about to make a clinical, psychological diagnosis of any ghost. But it was true that some—many even—were dangerous. Murderous. The crazy ones were worth the most.

"Hard to say. I mean, they're dead. Imagine what that does to your mental health. You die, you come back, but not quite."

"Right," Bothwell said with a nod. "So do they have to resolve unfinished business before moving on or something?"

"What?"

"Like in movies? Like if he solved his murder, would his spirit get to rest?"

"I don't think it works like that," Tate said. He pressed the red button, and the box closed. The ghost vanished, sealed in by whatever properties lead had to keep ghostly energy trapped. He punched in the code and opened the door, retrieving the sealed box and handing it to Bothwell.

"Please, just tell Connor this is getting out of hand. If he wants to increase the ghosts, I'm pulling out of this place. I either need more help or less junk getting shipped here."

"I'll see what I can do," Bothwell said dismissively. He took the box in one hand and left without another word. Tate watched him go and shook his head.

Since Connor had taken over the Endless Night, they had significantly ramped up the production of ghosts, and the potential for huge money was just around the corner. They just needed to get themselves organized.

But no one listened to Tate. Just the dead.

---

If you enjoyed the book, please leave a review. Your reviews inspire us to continue writing about the world of spooky and untold horrors!

Check out these best-selling books from our talented authors

### Ron Ripley (Ghost Stories)
- Berkley Street Series Books 1 – 9
  www.scarestreet.com/berkleyfullseries
- Moving in Series Box Set Books 1 – 6
  www.scarestreet.com/movinginboxfull

### A. I. Nasser (Supernatural Suspense)
- Slaughter Series Books 1 – 3 Bonus Edition
  www.scarestreet.com/slaughterseries

### David Longhorn (Sci-Fi Horror)
- Nightmare Series: Books 1 – 3
  www.scarestreet.com/nightmarebox
- Nightmare Series: Books 4 – 6
  www.scarestreet.com/nightmare4-6

### Sara Clancy (Supernatural Suspense)
- Banshee Series Books 1 – 6
  www.scarestreet.com/banshee1-6

For a complete list of our new releases and best-selling horror books, visit www.scarestreet.com/books

See you in the shadows,
Team Scare Street

Printed in Great Britain
by Amazon